She'd spoken to the boy, and her soft voice had hit him like a blow to the stomach.

While he might not have recognized her body or face, he could not mistake that voice as hers; her voice had haunted him, too. Before he could recover, he turned his attention to the child, and reeled from another blow. With his curly black hair and dark green eyes, the child was even more recognizable than the woman. He looked exactly like the few childhood photos of Brendan that his stepmother hadn't managed to *accidentally* destroy.

He didn't even remember closing the distance between them, didn't remember reaching for her. But he held her, his hand wrapped tightly around her delicate wrist.

She lifted her face to him, and he saw it now—in the almond shape and silvery green color of her eyes. What he didn't recognize was the fear that widened those eyes and stole the color from her face.

"Josie...?"

LISA CHILDS

ROYAL RESCUE

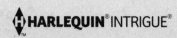

HARLEQUIN® INTRIGUE®

To Philip Tyson for proving to me that heroes really do exist!
Thank you for being my white knight!

Recycling programs
for this product may
not exist in your area.

ISBN-13: 978-0-373-69684-0

ROYAL RESCUE

Printed in U.S.A.

www.Harlequin.com

ABOUT THE AUTHOR

Bestselling, award-winning author Lisa Childs writes paranormal and contemporary romance for Harlequin Books. She lives on thirty acres in Michigan with her two daughters, a talkative Siamese and a long-haired Chihuahua who thinks she's a rottweiler. Lisa loves hearing from readers, who can contact her through her website, www.lisachilds.com, or snail-mail address, P.O. Box 139, Marne, MI 49435.

Books by Lisa Childs

HARLEQUIN INTRIGUE
 664—RETURN OF THE LAWMAN
 720—SARAH'S SECRETS
 758—BRIDAL RECONNAISSANCE
 834—THE SUBSTITUTE SISTER
1213—MYSTERY LOVER
1263—RANSOM FOR A PRINCE
1318—DADDY BOMBSHELL
1338—LAWMAN LOVER*
1344—BABY BREAKOUT*
1403—PROTECTING THE PREGNANT PRINCESS**
1410—THE PRINCESS PREDICAMENT**
1417—ROYAL RESCUE**

*Outlaws
**Royal Bodyguards

CAST OF CHARACTERS

Josie Jessup—Known to some as JJ Brandt, she's the American princess who died over three years ago. With the help of a U.S. marshal, Josie staged her death in order to save her life and the life of her unborn child. Lured out of hiding, she puts herself and her son in danger.

Brendan O'Hannigan—The father of Josie's child has the most reasons to want her dead, but the mobster's son isn't who everyone—including Josie—believes him to be. While he wants to rescue Josie and the son he didn't realize he had, his secret mission might put them in more danger.

Charlie "CJ" Brandt—The three-year-old boy loves his mother and wants to protect her from all the "bad" men, never realizing that one of them might be his father.

Stanley Jessup—An attempt on the media mogul's life is what lures his daughter out of hiding, but the powerful man has many enemies who might go after Josie and her son out of vengeance.

Margaret O'Hannigan—Brendan's stepmother wants control of the family business and fortune, and she isn't above eliminating all of her dead husband's heirs.

U.S. Marshal Donald Peterson—Does the man intend to relocate Josie for her protection or for her peril?

Chapter One

Goose bumps of dread rising on her arms, Josie Jessup slipped into a pew in the back of church. She hated funerals, hated saying goodbye to anyone but most especially to someone who had died too soon. And so senselessly and violently—shot down just as his adult life was beginning.

The small church, with its brilliantly colored stained-glass windows, was filled with her former student's family and friends. Some of them nodded in polite acknowledgment; others glared at her. They probably blamed her for the career he had pursued, the career that had cost him his life. At the local community college where she taught journalism courses, she had recognized the kid's talent. She had even recommended he cover the story that had killed him, because it had been killing her that she couldn't cover it herself.

But she couldn't risk anyone recognizing her. Even though her appearance had changed, her writing style hadn't. If she had written the story, certain people would have recognized it as hers no matter whom the byline claimed had authored it. And Josie couldn't risk anyone realizing that she wasn't really dead.

That was her other reason for hating funerals—

because it reminded her of her own, of having to say goodbye to everyone she loved. She actually hadn't attended her funeral; her ashes hadn't been in the urn as everyone else had believed. But still she'd had to say goodbye to the only life she'd known in order to begin a new life under a new identity.

But apparently she wasn't making any better choices in this life than she had in her last, since innocent people were still getting hurt. She hadn't pulled the trigger and ended this young man's promising life. But she blamed herself nearly as much as some of these people blamed her. If only she hadn't mentioned her suspicions regarding the private psychiatric hospital and the things that were rumored to take place there…

The gnawing pangs of guilt were all too familiar to her. The first story she'd covered, back in college, had also cost a young man his life. But then she'd had someone to assure her that it wasn't her fault. Now she had no one to offer her assurances or comfort.

Chatter from the people in front of her drifted back. "Since Michael was hoping to sell the Serenity House story to one of Jessup Media's news outlets, I heard Stanley Jessup might attend the funeral."

Josie's breath caught with hope and panic. She wanted to see him. But she couldn't risk his *seeing* her. For his own protection, her father had to go on believing that his only child was dead.

"Not anymore," the other person responded. "He's in the hospital. They don't even know if he'll make it."

Josie leaned forward, ready to demand to know what had happened to her father. But before she could, the other person had already asked.

"He was attacked," the gossiper replied. "Someone tried to kill him."

Had all the sacrifices she'd made been for naught? Had her father been attacked because of her? And if so, then she'd done nothing to protect him except deprive him of what mattered most to him. She had already been guilt-ridden. Now that guilt intensified, overwhelming her.

If her father didn't make it, he would die never knowing the truth. She couldn't let that happen.

"JESSUP…HOSPITALIZED in critical condition…"

The breaking news announcement drew Brendan O'Hannigan's attention to the television mounted over the polished oak-and-brass bar of O'Hannigan's Tavern. At 9:00 a.m. it was too early for the establishment to be open to the public, but it was already doing business. Another kind of business than serving drinks or sandwiches. A dangerous kind of business that required his entire focus and control.

But Brendan ignored the men with whom he was meeting to listen to the rest of the report: "Nearly four years ago, media mogul Stanley Jessup's daughter died in a house explosion that authorities ruled arson. Despite her father's substantial resources, Josie Jessup's murder has never been solved."

"Josie Jessup?" one of the men repeated her name and then tapped the table in front of Brendan. "Weren't you dating her at one time?"

Another of the men snorted. "A reporter? Brendan would never date a reporter."

He cleared his throat, fighting back all the emotions just the sound of her name evoked. And it had been more than three years.…

Wasn't it supposed to get easier? Weren't his memories of her supposed to fade? He shouldn't be able to see her as clearly as if she stood before him now, her pale green eyes sparkling and her long red hair flowing around her shoulders. Brendan could even hear her laughter tinkling in his ear.

"At the time I didn't know she was a reporter," he answered honestly, even though these were men he shouldn't trust with the truth. Hell, he shouldn't trust these men with anything.

He leaned back against the booth, and its stiff vinyl pushed the barrel of his gun into the small of his back. The bite of metal reassured him. It was just one of the many weapons he carried. That reassured him more.

The first man who'd spoken nodded and confirmed, "It wasn't common knowledge that the girl wanted to work for her father. All her life she had seemed more intent on spending his money, living the life of an American princess."

An American princess. That was exactly what Josie had been. Rich and spoiled, going after what she wanted no matter who might get hurt. She had hurt others—with the stories Brendan had discovered that she'd written under a pseudonym. Her exposés had started before she'd even graduated with her degree in journalism.

Brendan should have dug deeper until he'd learned the truth about her before getting involved with her. But the woman had pursued him and had been damn hard to resist. At least he had learned the truth about her before she'd managed to learn the truth about him. Somehow she must have discovered enough information to have gotten herself killed, though.

The news report continued: "The death of his daughter nearly destroyed Jessup, but the billionaire used his work to overcome his loss, much as he did when his wife died twenty years ago. The late Mrs. Jessup was European royalty."

"So she was a real princess," Brendan murmured, correcting himself.

"She was also a reporter," the other man said, his focus on Brendan, his dark eyes narrowed with suspicion.

It had taken Brendan four years to gain the small amount of trust and acceptance that he had from these men. He had been a stranger to them when he'd taken over the business he'd inherited from his late father. And these men didn't trust strangers.

Hell, they didn't trust anyone.

The man asked, "When did you learn that?"

Learn that Josie Jessup had betrayed him? That she'd just been using him to get another exposé for her father's media outlets?

Anger coursed through him and he clenched his jaw. His eyes must have also telegraphed that rage, for the men across the booth from him leaned back now as if trying to get away. Or to reassure themselves that they were armed, too.

"I found out Josie Jessup was a reporter," Brendan said, "right before she died."

It's too great a risk... She hadn't been able to reach her handler, the former U.S. marshal who had faked Josie's death and relocated her. But she didn't need to speak to Charlotte Green to know what she would have told her. *It's too great a risk...*

After nearly being killed for real almost four years ago, Josie knew how much danger she would be in were anyone to discover that she was still alive. She hadn't tried to call Charlotte again. She'd had no intention of listening to her anyway.

Josie stood outside her father's private hospital room, one hand pressed against the door. Coming here was indeed a risk, but the greater risk was that her father would die without her seeing him again.

Without him seeing her again. And…

Her hand that was not pressed against the door held another hand. Pudgy little fingers wriggled in her grasp. "Mommy, what we doin' here?"

Josie didn't have to ask herself that question. She knew that, no matter what the risk, she needed to be here. She needed to introduce her father to his grandson. "We're here to see your grandpa," she said.

"Grampa?" The three-year-old's little brow furrowed in confusion. He had probably heard the word before but never in reference to any relation of his. It had always been only the two of them. "I have a grampa?"

"Yes," Josie said. "But he lives far away so we didn't get to see him before now."

"Far away," he agreed with a nod and a yawn. He had slept through most of the long drive from northwestern Michigan to Chicago; his soft snoring had kept her awake and amused. His bright red curls were matted from his booster seat, and there was a trace of drool that had run from the corner of his mouth across his freckled cheek.

CJ glanced nervously around the wide corridor as if just now realizing where he was. He hadn't awakened until the elevator ride up to her father's floor. Then with protests that he wasn't a baby but a big boy now, he had wriggled out of her arms. "Does Grampa live here?"

"No," she said. "This is a hospital."

The little boy shuddered in revulsion. His low pain threshold for immunizations had given him a deep aversion to all things medical. He lowered his already soft voice to a fearful whisper. "Is—is Grampa sick?"

She whispered, too, so that nobody overheard them. A few hospital workers, men dressed in scrubs, lingered outside a room a few doors down from her father's. "He's hurt."

So where were the police or the security guards? Why was no one protecting him?

Because nobody cared about her father the way she did. Because she had been declared dead, he had no other next of kin. And as powerful and intimidating a man as he was, he had no genuine friends, either. His durable power of attorney was probably held by his lawyer. She'd claimed to be from his office when she'd called to find out her father's room number.

"Did he falled off his bike?" CJ asked.

"Something like that." She couldn't tell her son what had really happened, that her father had been assaulted in the parking garage of his condominium complex. Usually the security was very high there. No one got through the gate unless they lived in the building. Not only was it supposed to be safe, but it was his home. Yet someone had attacked him, striking him with something—a baseball bat or a pipe. His broken arm and bruised shoulder might not hurt him so badly if the assault hadn't also brought on a heart attack.

Would her showing up here as if from the dead bring on another one? Maybe that inner voice of hers, which sounded a hell of a lot like Charlotte's even though she hadn't talked to the woman, was right. The risk was too great.

"We shoulda brought him ice cream," CJ said. "Ice cream makes you feel all better."

Every time he had been brave for his shots she had rewarded him with ice cream. Always shy and nervous, CJ had to fight hard to be brave. Had she passed her own fears, of discovery and danger, onto her son?

"Yes, we should have," she agreed, and she pulled her hand away from the door. "We should do that…"

"Now?" CJ asked, his dark bluish-green eyes brightening with hope. "We gonna get ice cream now?"

"It's too late for ice cream tonight," she said. "But we can get some tomorrow."

"And bring it back?"

She wasn't sure about that. She would have to pose as the legal secretary again and learn more about her father's condition. Just how fragile was his health?

Josie turned away from the door and from the nearly overwhelming urge to run inside and into her father's arms—the way she always had as a child. She had hurled herself at him, secure that he would catch her.

She'd been so confident that he would always be there for her. She had never considered that he might be the one to leave—for real, for good—that he might be the one to really die. Given how young she was when her mother died, she should have understood how fragile life was. But her father wasn't fragile. He was strong and powerful. Invincible. Or so she had always believed.

But he wasn't. And she couldn't risk causing him harm only to comfort herself. She stepped away from the door, but her arm jerked as her son kept his feet planted on the floor.

"I wanna see Grampa," he said, his voice still quiet but his tone determined. Afraid to draw attention to

himself, her son had never thrown a temper tantrum.
He'd never even raised his voice. But he could be very
stubborn when he put his mind to something. Kind of
like the grandfather he'd suddenly decided he needed
to meet.

"It's late," she reminded him. "He'll be sleeping and
we shouldn't wake him up."

His little brow still furrowed, he stared up at her a
moment as if considering her words. Then he nodded.
"Yeah, you get cranky when I wake you up."

A laugh sputtered out of her lips. Anyone would get
cranky if woken up at 5:00 a.m. to watch cartoons. "So
we better make sure I get some sleep tonight." That
meant postponing the drive back and getting a hotel.
But she needed to be close to the hospital…in case her
father took a turn for the worse. In case he needed her.

"And after you wake up we'll come back with ice
cream?"

She hesitated before offering him a slight nod. But
instead of posing as the lawyer's assistant again, she
would talk to Charlotte.

Someone else had answered the woman's phone at
the palace on the affluent island country of St. Pierre
where Charlotte had gone to work as the princess's
bodyguard after leaving the U.S. Marshals. That person
had assured Josie that Charlotte would be back soon to
return her call. But Josie hadn't left a message—she
couldn't trust anyone but Charlotte with her life. Or
her father's. She would talk to Charlotte and see what
the former marshal could find out about Josie's father's condition and the attack. Then she would come
back to see him.

Her son accepted her slight nod as agreement and
finally moved away from the door to his grandfather's

room. "Does Grampa like 'nilla ice cream or chocolate or cookie dough or…"

The kid was an ice-cream connoisseur, his list of flavors long and impressive. And Josie's stomach nearly growled with either hunger or nerves.

She interrupted him to ask, "Do you want to press the elevator button?"

His brow furrowing in concentration, he rose up on tiptoe and reached for the up arrow.

"No," she said. But it was too late, he'd already pressed it. "We need the down arrow." Before she could touch it, a hand wrapped around her wrist.

Her skin tingled and her pulse leaped in reaction. And she didn't need to lift her head to know who had touched her. Even after more than three years, she recognized his touch. But she lifted her head and gazed up at him, at his thick black hair that was given to curl, at his deep, turquoise-green eyes that could hold such passion. Now they held utter shock and confusion.

This was the man who'd killed her, or who would have killed her had the U.S. marshal and one of her security guards not diffused the bomb that had been set inside the so-called *safe* house. They had set it off later to stage her death.

Since he had wanted her dead so badly, he was not going to be happy to find her alive and unharmed— if he recognized her now. She needed for him *not* to recognize her, as she wasn't likely to survive his next murder attempt. Not when she was unprotected.

If only she'd listened to that inner voice…

The risk had been too great. Not just to her life but to what would become of her son once she was gone.

Would her little boy's father take him or kill him? Either way, the child was as doomed as she was.

Chapter Two

For more than three years, her memory had haunted Brendan—her image always in his mind. This woman didn't look like her, but she had immediately drawn his attention when he'd stepped out of the stairwell at the end of the hall. Her body was fuller and softer than Josie's thin frame had been. And her chin-length blond bob had nothing in common with Josie's long red hair. Yet something about her—the way she tilted her jaw, the sparkle in her eyes as she gazed down at the child—reminded him of her.

Then she'd spoken to the boy, and her soft voice had hit him like a blow to the stomach. While he might not have recognized her body or face, he could not mistake that voice as anyone's but hers. Her voice had haunted him, too.

Before he could recover, he turned his attention to the child and reeled from another blow. With his curly red hair and bright green eyes, the child was more recognizable than the woman. Except for that shock of bright hair, he looked exactly like the few childhood photos of Brendan that his stepmother hadn't managed to *accidentally* destroy.

He didn't even remember closing the distance between them, didn't remember reaching for her. But now he held her, his hand wrapped tightly around her delicate wrist.

She lifted her face to him, and he saw it now in the almond shape and silvery-green color of her eyes. What he didn't recognize was the fear that widened those eyes and stole the color from her face.

"Josie…?"

She shook her head in denial.

She must have had some cosmetic work done, because her appearance was different. Her cheekbones weren't as sharp, her chin not as pointy, her nose not as perfectly straight. This plastic surgeon had done the opposite of what was usually required; he'd made her perfect features imperfect—made her look less movie-star gorgeous and more natural.

Why would she have gone to such extremes to change her identity? With him, her effort was wasted. He would know her anywhere, just from the way his body reacted—tensing and tingling with attraction. And anger. But she was already afraid of him and he didn't want to scare the child, too, so he restrained his rage over her cruel deception.

"You're Josie Jessup."

She shook her head again and spoke, but this time her voice was little more than a raspy whisper. "You're mistaken. That's not my name."

The raspy whisper did nothing to disguise her voice, since it was how he best remembered her. A raspy whisper in his ear as they'd made love, his body thrusting into hers, hers arching to take him deep. Her nails digging into his shoulders and back as she'd screamed his name.

That was why he'd let her fool him once, why he'd

let her distract him when he had needed to be focused
and careful. She had seduced and manipulated him
with all her loving lies. She'd only wanted to get close
to him so she could get a damn story. She hadn't realized how dangerous getting close to him really was. No
matter what she'd learned, she didn't know the truth
about him. And if he had anything to say about it, she
never would. He wouldn't let her make a fool of him
twice.

"If you're not Josie Jessup, what the—" He swallowed a curse for the child's sake. "What are you doing
here?"

"We were gonna see my grampa," the little boy answered for her, "but we didn't wanna wake him up."

She was the same damn liar she had always been,
but at least she hadn't corrupted the boy.

His son...

JOSIE RESISTED THE urge to press her palm over CJ's
mouth. It was already too late. Why was it *now* that
her usually shy son chose to speak to a stranger? And,
moreover, to speak the truth? But her little boy was
unfailingly honest, no matter the fact that his mother
couldn't be. Especially now.

"But we got out on the wrong floor," she said. "This
isn't where your grandfather's room is."

CJ shook his head. "No, we watched the numbers
lighting up in the el'vator. You said number six. I know
my numbers."

Now she cursed herself for working with the three-
year-old so much that he knew all his numbers and let-
ters. "Well, it's the wrong room."

"You said number—"

"Shh, sweetheart, you're tired and must not remember correctly," she said, hoping that her son picked up the warning and the fear in her voice now. "We need to leave. It's late. We need to get you to bed."

But those strong masculine fingers were still wrapped tight around her wrist. "You're not going anywhere."

"You have no right to keep me," she said.

With his free hand, he gestured toward CJ. "He gives me the right. I have a lot of rights you've apparently denied me."

"I—I don't know what you're talking about." Why the hell would she have told the man who'd tried to kill her that she was pregnant with his baby? If his attempts had been successful, he would have killed them both.

"You know exactly what I'm talking about, Josie."

CJ tugged on her hand and whispered loudly, "Mommy, why does the man keep calling you that?"

Now he supported her lie—too late. "I don't know, honey," she said. "He has me mixed up with someone else he must have known."

"No," Brendan said. "I never really knew Josie Jessup at all."

No. He hadn't. Or he would have realized that she was too smart to have ever really trusted him. If only she'd been too smart to fall for him...

But the man was as charming as he was powerful. And when he'd touched her, when he'd kissed her, she had been unable to resist that charm.

"Then it's no wonder that you've mistaken me for her," Josie said, "since you didn't really know her very well."

She furrowed her brow and acted as if a thought had just occurred to her. "Josie Jessup? Isn't that the daughter of the media mogul? I thought she died several years ago."

"That was obviously what she wanted everyone to believe—that she was dead," he said. "Or was it just me?"

She shrugged. "I wouldn't know." *You. Just you.* But unfortunately, for him to accept the lie, everyone else had had to believe it, too. "I am not her. She must really be gone."

And if she'd had any sense, she would have stayed gone. Well away from her father and this man.

"Why are *you* here?" she asked. "Are you visiting someone?"

Or knowing all this time that she wasn't really dead, had he set a trap for her? Was he the one who had attacked her father? According to the reports from all her father's media outlets, there was no suspect yet in his assault. But she had one now.

She needed to call Charlotte. But the phone was in her purse, and she had locked her purse in her vehicle so that if anyone was to recognize her, they wouldn't be able to find her new identity.

"It doesn't matter why I'm here—just that I am," he said, dodging her question as he had so many other questions she had asked him during the months they'd been together. "And so are you."

"Not anymore. We're leaving," she said, as much to CJ as to Brendan. As if on cue, the elevator ground to a stop, and the doors slid open. She moved to step into the car, but her wrist was clutched so tightly she couldn't move.

"That one's going up," Brendan pointed out.

"As I said, we got off on the wrong floor." She tugged hard on her wrist, but his grip didn't ease. She didn't want to scream and alarm her already trembling son, so through gritted teeth she said, "Let go of me."

But he stepped closer. He was so damn big, all broad muscles and tension. There were other bulges beneath the jacket of his dark tailored suit—weapons. He had always carried guns. He'd told her it was because of the dangerous people who resented his inheriting his father's businesses.

But she'd wondered then if he'd been armed for protection or intimidation. She was intimidated, so intimidated that she cared less about scaring her son than she did about protecting him. So she screamed.

HER SCREAM STARTLED Brendan and pierced the quiet of the hospital corridor. But he didn't release her until her son—*their* son—launched himself at Brendan. His tiny feet kicked at Brendan's shins and his tiny fists flailed, striking Brendan's thighs and hips.

"Leggo my mommy! Leggo my mommy!"

The boy's reaction and fear startled Brendan into stepping back. Josie's wrist slipped from his grasp. She used her freed hand to catch their son's flailing fists and tug him close to her.

Before Brandon could reach for her again, three men dressed in hospital scrubs rushed up from the room they'd been loitering near down the hall. Brendan had noted their presence but had been too distracted to realize that they were watching him.

Damn! He had been trained to constantly be aware of his surroundings and everyone in them. Only Josie had ever made him forget his training to trust no one.

"What's going on?" one of the men asked.

"This man accosted me and my son," Josie replied, spewing more lies. "He tried to grab me."

Brendan struggled to control his anger. The boy—his boy—was already frightened of him. He couldn't add to that fear by telling the truth. So he stepped back again in order to appear nonthreatening, when all he wanted to do was threaten.

"We'll escort you to your car, ma'am," another of the men offered as he guided her and the child into the waiting elevator.

"Don't let her leave," Brendan advised. Because if she left, he had no doubt that he would never see her and his son again. This time she would stay gone. He moved forward, reaching for those elevator doors before they could shut on Josie and their son.

But strong hands closed around his arms, dragging him back, while another man joined Josie inside the elevator. Just as the doors slid shut, Brendan noticed the telltale bulge of a weapon beneath the man's scrubs. He carried a gun at the small of his back.

Brendan shrugged off the grasp of the man who held him. Then he whirled around to face him. But now he faced down the barrel of his gun. Why were he and at least one of the other men armed? They weren't hospital security, and he doubted like hell that they were orderlies.

Who were they? And more important, who had sent them?

The guy warned Brendan, "Don't be a hero, man."

He laughed incredulously at the idea of anyone considering *him* a hero. "Do you know who I am?"

"I don't care who the hell you are," the guy replied, as he cocked the gun, "and neither will this bullet."

Four years ago Brendan's father had learned that it didn't matter who he was, either. When he'd been shot in the alley behind O'Hannigan's early one morning, that bullet had made him just as dead as anyone else who got shot. Even knowing the dangerous life his father had led, his murder had surprised Brendan.

As the old man had believed himself invincible, so had Brendan. Or maybe he just remembered being fifteen, running away from the strong, ruthless man and never looking back.

But Dennis O'Hannigan's death had brought Brendan back to Chicago and to the life he'd sworn he'd never live. Most people thought he'd come home to claim his inheritance. Even now he couldn't imagine why the old man had left everything to him.

They hadn't spoken in more than fifteen years, even though his father had known where Brendan was and what he'd been doing. No one had ever been able to hide from Dennis O'Hannigan—not his friends or his family and certainly not his enemies.

Which one had ended the old man's life?

Brendan had really returned to claim justice. No matter how ruthless his father had been, he deserved to have his murder solved, his killer punished.

Some people thought Brendan had committed the murder—out of vengeance and greed. He had certainly had reasons for wanting revenge. His father had been as cruel a father and husband as he'd been a crime boss.

And as a crime boss, the man had acquired a fortune—a destiny and a legacy that he'd left to his only blood relative. Because, since his father's death, Brendan was the only O'Hannigan left in the family. Or so he'd thought until he'd met his son tonight.

He couldn't lose the boy before he even got to know him. No matter how many people thought of him as a villain, he would have to figure out a way to be the hero.

He had to save his son.

And Josie.

Four years ago she must have realized that she was in danger—that must have been why she'd staged her own death. Had she realized yet that those men in the elevator with her were not orderlies or interns but dangerous gunmen? Had she realized that she was in as much or more danger now than she'd been in before?

Chapter Three

Fear gripped Josie. She was more scared now than she'd been when Brendan wouldn't let go of her. Maybe her pulse raced and her heart hammered just in reaction to his discovering her. Or maybe it was because she wasn't entirely certain she had really gotten away from him...even as the doors slid closed between them.

"Thank you," she told the men. "I really appreciate your helping me and my son to safety."

"Was that man threatening you?" one of them asked.

She nodded. More threatening than they could possibly understand. Brendan O'Hannigan could take even more from her now than just her life. He could take away her son.

"H-he's a b-bad man," CJ stammered. The little boy trembled with fear and the aftereffects of his physical defense of his mother.

"Are you okay?" she asked him, concerned that he'd gotten hurt when he'd flung himself at Brendan. She couldn't believe her timid son had summoned that much courage and anger. And she hated that she'd been so careless with their safety that she'd put him in such a dangerous predicament. Dropping to her knees in front of her son, she inspected him to see if he had been harmed.

His little face was flushed nearly as bright red as his tousled curls. His eyes glistened with tears he was fighting hard not to shed. He blinked furiously and bit his bottom lip. Even at three, he was too proud to cry in front of strangers. He nodded.

Her heart clutched in her chest, aching with love and pride. "You were so brave." She wound her arms tightly around him and lifted him up as she stood again. Maybe a good parent would have admonished him for physically launching himself at a stranger. But it was so hard for him to be courageous that she had to praise his efforts. "Thank you for protecting Mommy."

She hadn't been able to shake Brendan's strong grip. But CJ's attack had caught the mobster off guard so that he'd released her and stepped back. She released a shuddery breath of relief that he hadn't hurt her son.

CJ wrapped his pudgy little legs around her waist and clung to her, his slight body trembling against her. "The bad man is gone?"

"He's gone."

But for how long? Had he just taken the stairs to meet the elevator when it stopped? CJ had pushed the up arrow, so the car was going to the roof. She doubted Brendan would waste his time going up. Instead he would have more time to get down to the lobby and lay in wait for her and CJ to leave for the parking garage.

And if he followed her there, she would have no protection against him. Unlike him, she carried no weapons. Just a can of mace and that was inside her purse, which she had locked in her vehicle.

But these men had promised to see her safely to her car. Surely they would protect her against Brendan…

But who would protect her from them?

The thought slipped unbidden into her mind, making her realize why her pulse hadn't slowed. She didn't feel safe yet.

Not with them.

Balancing CJ on her hip and holding him with just one arm, she reached for the panel of buttons. But one of the men stepped in front of it, blocking her from the lobby or the emergency call button. Then the other man stepped closer to her, trapping her and CJ between them.

She clutched her son more closely to her chest and glanced up at the illuminated numbers above the doors. They were heading toward the roof. Why hadn't they pushed other buttons to send the car back down? These men would have no patients to treat up there. But then, just because they wore scrubs didn't mean that they actually worked at the hospital.

When Charlotte had relocated her more than three years ago, she'd taught Josie to trust no one but her. And her own instincts. She should have heeded that warning before she'd stepped inside the elevator with these men. She should have heeded that warning before she'd driven back to Chicago.

"My son and I need to leave," she said, wishing now that she had never left her safe little home in Michigan. But she'd been so worried about her father that she'd listened to her heart instead of her head.

"That's the plan, Miss Jessup," the one standing in front of the elevator panel replied. "To get you out of here."

Somehow she suspected he wasn't talking about just getting her out of the hospital. And, like Brendan, he had easily recognized her.

She should have heeded Charlotte's other advice all those years ago to have more plastic surgery. But Josie had stopped when she'd struggled to recognize her own face in the mirror. She hadn't wanted to forget who she was. But maybe she should have taken that risk. It was definitely safer than the risk she'd taken in coming to see her father.

She feared that risk was going to wind up costing her everything.

"COME ON, GUY, just walk away," the pseudo-orderly advised Brendan.

"You don't want to shoot me," Brendan warned, stepping closer to the man instead of walking away. That had always been his problem. Once he got out of trouble, the way he had when he'd run away nearly twenty years ago, he turned around and headed right back into it—even deeper than before.

The other man shrugged. "Doesn't matter to me. The security cameras are not functioning up here."

Brendan suspected that had been intentional. While he had been completely shocked to see Josie, these men had been expecting her. They had actually been waiting for her…with disabled security cameras and weapons.

So Stanley Jessup's assault hadn't been such a random act of violence. It was the trap that had been used to draw Josie out of hiding.

Was he the only one who hadn't known that she was really alive?

"And Jessup, who's heavily drugged, is the only patient in a room near here. So by the time someone responds to the sound of the shot," the man brazenly bragged, "I'll be gone. We planned our escape route."

Brendan needed to plan his, too. But he didn't intend to escape danger. He planned to confront it head-on and eliminate the threat.

"In fact," the man continued, his ruddy face contorting with a smirk, "it would be better to kill you than leave you behind as a potential witness." He lifted the gun, so there was no way the bullet would miss. Then he cocked the trigger.

Brendan had a gun, too, holstered under his arm. And another at his back. And one strapped to his ankle. But before he could pull any of them, he would have a bullet in his head. So instead of fighting with a weapon, he used his words.

"I'm Brendan O'Hannigan," he said, "and that's why you don't want to shoot me."

First the man snorted derisively as if the name meant nothing to him. Then he repeated it, "O'Hannigan," as if trying to place where he'd heard it before. Then his eyes widened and his jaw dropped open as recognition struck him with the same force as if Brendan had swung his fist at him. "Oh, shit."

That was how people usually reacted when they learned his identity—except for Josie. She had acted as if she'd known nothing of his family or their dubious family business. And she had gotten close to him, with her impromptu visits to the tavern and her persistent flirting, before he'd realized that she had been doing just that: acting.

She had known exactly who he was or she would have never sought him out. She'd been after a scoop for her father's media outlets. Even after all those other stories she'd brought to him, she'd still been trying to prove herself to *Daddy*.

Brendan had devoted himself to just the opposite, trying to prove himself as unlike his father as possible.

Until the old man had died, drawing Brendan back into a life that he had been unable to run far enough away from when he was a kid.

"Yeah, if you shoot me, you better hope the police find you before any of my family does," Brendan warned the man. But it was a bluff.

He really had no idea what his "family" would do or if they would even care. He was the only one who cared about his father's murder—enough to risk everything for justice. Hell, his "family," given the way they'd resented his return and his inheritance, would probably be relieved if he died, especially if they knew the truth about him.

The man stepped back and lifted his gun so that the barrel pointed toward the ceiling, waving it around as if there were a white flag of surrender tied to the end of it. "I don't want any trouble—any of *your* kind of trouble."

Brendan didn't want that kind of trouble, either. But it was too late. He was in too deep now—so deep that he hadn't been able to get out even after he'd thought Josie had been killed. But then her death had made him even more determined to pursue justice.

"If you didn't want trouble," Brendan said, "then you shouldn't have messed with my son and his mother." Now he swung his fist into the man's face.

The guy fell back, but before he went down, Brendan snapped the gun from his grasp and turned it on him. There was no greater power play than turning a man's own gun on him. His father had taught him that, starting his lessons when Brendan was only a few years older than his son was now.

"What the hell do you want with her?" he demanded.

"I just got paid to do a job, man," the man in scrubs said, cringing away from the barrel pointed in his face.

"What's the job?"

The man opened his mouth but hesitated before speaking, until Brendan cocked the trigger. Then he blurted out, "To kill Josie Jessup!"

"Damn it!" he cursed at having his suspicions confirmed.

He had only just discovered that she was alive and that she'd given birth to his son. He didn't want to lose the boy before he'd gotten the chance to claim him. And he didn't want Josie to die again. He glanced back at the elevator, at the numbers above the doors that indicated it had stopped—on the top floor.

"You're not going to make it," the man advised. "You're not going to be able to save her."

Brendan cursed again because the guy was probably right. But still he had to try. He turned the gun and swung the handle at the man's head.

One down. Two to go...

THE WIND ON the roof was cold, whipping through Josie's light jacket and jeans. She slipped the side of her unzipped jacket over CJ's back to shield him from the cold bite of the breeze. He snuggled against her, his face pressed into her neck. Her skin was damp from the quiet tears he surreptitiously shed. He must have felt the fear and panic that clutched at her, and he trembled with it while she tensely held herself together.

She had to do something. She had to make certain these men didn't hurt her son. But since she hadn't reached Charlotte, earlier, the former U.S. marshal couldn't come to her rescue as she had last time. Josie had only herself—and the instincts she'd previously ignored—to help her now.

The two men were huddled together just a few feet away from them, between her and CJ and the elevator. There was no way to reach it without going through them. And with the bulges of weapons at their backs, she didn't dare try to go through them. Nor did she want to risk turning her back on them to run, for fear that they would shoot. And since they were on the roof, where could she go? How far could she run without falling over the side?

One of the men spoke into a cell phone about the change in plans: *CJ.*

While they had somehow discovered that she was really alive, they must not have been aware that she was pregnant when she'd gone into hiding.

Despite the fact that he'd lowered his voice, it carried on the wind, bringing the horrifying words to her.

"…never agreed to do a kid."

"…someone else knows she's alive and hassled her in the hall."

Because Brendan wasn't any happier she was alive than these men apparently were. Of course he hadn't seemed as eager to rectify that as they were.

"Okay, I understand," said the man holding the phone before he clicked it off and slid it back into his pocket. Then he turned to his co-conspirator and nodded. "We have to eliminate them both."

A shudder of fear and revulsion rippled through Josie. Thankfully CJ wouldn't understand what they meant by "eliminate." But eventually he would figure it out, when he stared down the barrel of a gun.

"I don't know what you're getting paid to do this," she addressed the men as they turned toward her. "But

I have money. Lots of money. I can pay you more than you're getting now."

The man who'd been on the phone chuckled bitterly. "We were warned you might make that offer. But you forfeited your access to that money when you faked your death, lady."

They were right. Josie Jessup's bank accounts and trust fund had closed when she'd *died*. And JJ Brandt's salary from the community college was barely enough to cover her rent, utilities and groceries. She had nothing in her savings account to offer them.

"My father would pay you," she said, "whatever you ask." But first they would have to prove to him that she was really alive. She hadn't dared step inside his room. What would happen if gunmen burst inside with her? The shock would surely bring on another heart attack—maybe a fatal one.

The men shared a glance, obviously debating her offer. But then one of them shook his head. "This is about more than money, lady."

"What is it about?" she asked.

As far she knew, Brendan was the only one with any reason to want her dead. If these men worked for him, they wouldn't have held him back from boarding the elevator with her. If they worked for him, they wouldn't have dared to touch him at all. She still couldn't believe that she had dared to touch him, that she'd dared to go near him even to pursue her story. The police had been unable to determine who had killed his father, the legendary crime boss, so she had vowed to find out if there was any truth to the rumors that Dennis O'Hannigan's runaway son had killed him out of revenge and greed.

She had found something else entirely. More than the story, she had been attracted to the man—the complex man who had been grieving the death of his estranged father while trying to take over his illicit empire. She had never found evidence proving Brendan was the killer, but he must have been worried that she'd discovered something. Why else would he have tried to kill her?

Just because he'd learned she'd been lying to him about what she really was? Maybe. He'd been furious with her—furious enough to want revenge. But if he wasn't behind this attempt to eliminate her, had he been behind that bomb planted more than three years ago?

Could she have been wrong about him?

"I have a right to know," she prodded, wanting the truth. That was her problem—she always wanted the truth. It was what had made her such a great reporter before she'd been forced to give it all up to save her life. But since it was probably her last chance to learn it, she wanted this truth more than she'd ever wanted any other. If not Brendan, who wanted her dead?

"It doesn't matter what it's about," one of the men replied.

She suspected he had no idea, either, that he was just doing what he had been paid to do.

"It's not going to change the outcome for you and your son," the fake orderly continued as he reached behind him and drew out his gun.

What about her father? Had he only been attacked to lure her out of hiding? Was he safe now?

If only her son was safe, too…

She covered the side of CJ's cold, damp face with her hand so that he wouldn't see the weapon. Then she turned, putting her body between the boy and the men. Her body wouldn't be enough to protect her son, though. Nothing could protect him now. "Please…"

But if the men wouldn't respond to bribes, they would have no use for begging, either. So she just closed her eyes and prayed as the first shot rang out.

Chapter Four

Was he too late?

As the elevator doors slid open, a shot rang out. But the bullet ricocheted off the back of the car near his head. Both men faced *him* with their guns raised. Maybe this had nothing to do with Josie.

Maybe the woman wasn't even really her and the boy not really even his son. Maybe it had all been an elaborate trap to lure him here—to his death. Plenty of people wanted him dead. That was why he usually had backup within gunshot range. But he hadn't wanted anyone to be aware of his visit to the bedside of a man he didn't really know but with whom he'd thought he'd shared a tragedy: Josie's death.

So nobody had known he was coming here. These men weren't after him, because the suspects he knew wouldn't have gone to such extremes to take him out; they wouldn't have had to. Whenever they dared to try to take him out, as they had his father, they knew where to find him—at O'Hannigan's. Inside the family tavern was where Josie had found him. He'd thought the little rich girl had just wandered into the wrong place with the wrong clientele, and he'd rescued her before any of his rough customers could accost her.

Just as he had intended to rescue her now. But both times he was the one who wound up needing to be rescued. Maybe he should have had backup even for this uncomfortable visit. With the elevator doors wide open, Brendan was a damn sitting duck, more so even than the woman and the boy. They might be able to escape. Seeing the fear on their faces, pale and stark in the light spilling out of the elevator, it was clear that they were in real danger and they knew it.

"Run!" he yelled at them.

She sprinted away, either in reaction to his command or in fear of him as well as the armed men. With her and the kid out of the line of fire, he raised the gun he'd taken off their co-conspirator.

But the men had divided their attention now. Standing back-to-back, one fired at him while the other turned his gun toward Josie.

The boy clutched tightly in her arms, she ran, disappearing into the shadows before any bullets struck her. But maybe running wasn't a good thing, given that the farther away she went, the thicker the shadows grew. The light from the elevator illuminated only a small circle of the rooftop around the open doors. The farther she ran, the harder it would be for her to see where the roof ended and the black abyss twenty stories above the ground began.

He ducked back into the elevator and flattened himself against the panel beside the doors. He could have closed those doors to protect himself. But then he couldn't protect Josie and the child. *His son...*

These men weren't just trying to kill the woman who was supposed to already be dead. They were trying to kill a helpless child.

An O'Hannigan.

His father would be turning over in his grave.

Despite his occasional violent behavior toward them, Dennis O'Hannigan had never really wanted his family harmed—at least not by anyone but him. Brendan didn't want his family harmed at all. He kept one finger on the button to hold open the doors. Then he leaned out and aimed the gun. And squeezed the trigger.

His shots drew all the attention to him. Bullets pinged off the brass handrail and shattered the smoky glass of the elevator car. The glass splintered and ricocheted like the bullets, biting into his skin like a swarm of bees.

His finger jerked off the button, and the doors began to close. But he couldn't leave Josie and the child alone up here with no protection. Despite the other man's warning, he had to play the hero. But it had been nearly four years since he'd been anything but the villain.

Had he gotten rusty? Would he be able to protect them? Or had his arrival put them in even more danger?

"THEY'RE ALL BAD men," CJ said, his voice high and squeaky with fear and panic. "They're bad! Bad!"

He was too young to have learned just how evil some people were. As his mother, Josie was supposed to protect him, but she'd endangered his life and his innocence. She had to do her best to keep her little boy a little boy until he had the time to grow into a man.

"Shh…" Josie cautioned him. "We need to be very quiet."

"So they don't find us?"

"First we have to find a hiding place." Which wouldn't be easy in a darkness so enveloping she could barely see the child she held tightly against her.

She had been able to see the shots—those brief flashes of gunpowder. She'd run from those flashes, desperate to keep her son safe. But now those shots were redirected toward Brendan, and running wouldn't keep CJ safe since she couldn't see where she was going. She moved quickly but carefully, testing her footing before she stepped forward.

"Are they shooting real bullets?" he asked.

To preserve that innocence she was afraid he was losing, she could have lied. But that lie could risk his life.

"They're real," she replied, aware that they'd come all too close to her and CJ. "That's why we need to find a place to hide until the police come."

Someone must have heard the shots and reported them by now. Help had to be on the way. Hopefully it would arrive in time to save her and her son. But what about Brendan? He had stepped into the middle of an attempted murder—a double homicide, actually. And he hadn't done it accidentally. He had tracked her to the roof, maybe to kill her himself. But perhaps he'd be the one to lose his life, since the men were now entirely focused on him.

She shuddered, the thought chilling her nearly as much as the cold wind that whipped around the unprotected rooftop.

"Let's go back there, Mommy," CJ said, lifting his hand, which caught her attention only because she felt the movement more than saw it.

"Where?" she asked.

"Behind those big metal things."

She peered in the direction he was pointing and finally noted the glint of some stray starlight off steel vents, probably exhaust pipes for the hospital's heating or cooling system. If only they could escape inside them…

But she could barely move around them, let alone find a way inside them. The openings were too high above the rooftop, towering over her. As she tried to squeeze around them, her hip struck the metal. She winced and swallowed a groan of pain. And hoped the men hadn't heard the telltale metallic clink.

"Shh, Mommy," CJ cautioned her. "We don't want the bad men to hear us."

"No, we don't," she agreed.

"They might find our hiding place."

"I'm not sure we can hide here," she whispered. She couldn't wedge them both between the massive pipes. The metal caught at her clothes and scraped her arms. "We can't fit."

"Let me try," he suggested. Before she could agree, he wriggled down from her arms and squeezed through the small space.

She reached through the blackness, trying to clutch at him, trying to pull him back. What if he'd fallen right off the building?

She had no idea how much space was on the other side of the pipes. A tiny ledge? None?

A scream burned in her throat, but she was too scared to utter it—too horrified that in trying to protect her son she may have lost him forever.

But then chubby fingers caught hers. He tugged on her hand. "Come on, Mommy. There's room."

"You're not at the edge of the roof?" she asked, worried that he might be in more danger where he was.

"Nooo," he murmured, his voice sounding as if he'd turned away from her. "There's a little wall right behind me."

"Don't go over that wall," she advised. It was probably the edge of the roof, a small ledge to separate the rooftop from the ground far below. A curious little boy might want to figure out what was on the other side of that wall.

"Okay, Mommy," he murmured again, his voice still muffled. Was he trying to peer over the side?

She needed to get to him, needed to protect him, from the men and from himself. She turned sideways and pushed herself against the space where CJ had so effortlessly disappeared. But her breasts and hips— curves she'd barely had until her pregnancy with him— caught. She sucked in her stomach, but it made no difference. She couldn't suck in her breasts or hips. "I can't fit."

CJ tugged harder on her hand. "C'mon, Mommy, it's a good hiding place."

"No, honey," she corrected him, her pulse tripping with fear that he'd go over the wall, "you need to come back out. We'll find another one."

But then she heard it. She tilted her head and listened harder. And still it was all she heard: silence. The shooting had stopped.

What did that mean?

Was Brendan dead? Were the men? Whoever had survived would be searching for her next—for her and her son. The silence broke, shattered by the scrape of a shoe against the asphalt roofing.

She sucked in a breath now—of fear. But it didn't make it any easier for her to squeeze through the small space. And maybe pulling CJ out wasn't the best idea, not when he was safe from the men.

She dropped his fingers. "You stay here," she said. "In the best hiding place."

"I wanna hide with you."

"I'll find a bigger hiding place," she said. "You need to stay here and play statue for me."

She had played the game as a kid when she'd pretended to be a statue, completely still and silent. On those mornings that CJ had woken her up at five, she'd taught him to play statue so she could sleep just a little longer. Now acting lifeless was perhaps the only way for CJ to stay alive.

The footfalls grew louder as someone drew closer. She had to get out of here, had to distract whoever it was from CJ's hiding place. But first she had to utter one more warning. "Don't come out for anyone but me."

Her son was such a good boy. So smart and so obedient. She didn't have to worry that anyone else would lure him out of hiding. She just had to make sure that she stayed alive, so that he would come out when it was safe. So she drew in a deep breath and headed off, moving as fast as she dared in the darkness. She glanced back, but night had swallowed those metal vent pipes and had swallowed her son. Would she be able to find him again, even if she eluded whoever had survived the earlier gun battle?

She would worry about finding him after she found a hiding spot for herself. But it was so dark she could barely see where she was going. So she wasn't surprised when she collided with a wall.

But this wasn't a short brick wall like the one CJ had found behind the pipes. This wall was broad and muscular and warm. Her hands tingled in reaction to the chest she touched, her palms pressed against the lapels of a suit. The other men had been wearing scrubs, which would have been scratchy and flat.

And she wouldn't have reacted this way to them. Her skin wouldn't tingle; her pulse wouldn't leap. And she wouldn't feel something very much like relief that he was alive. No matter what threat he posed to her, she hadn't wanted him dead.

"Brendan...?"

IT WAS HER. Despite her physical transformation, he'd recognized her. But now he had not even a fraction of a doubt. That voice in the darkness...

Her touch...

He recognized all that about her, too.

But more importantly, *she* had recognized *him*. If she was truly a stranger that he had mistaken for his former lover and betrayer, she wouldn't know his name. Or, if by some chance, she had just recognized him as the son of a notorious mobster, she wouldn't have been comfortable and familiar enough to call him by his first name.

"Yes, Josie, it's me," he assured her.

She shuddered and her hands began to tremble against his chest. "You—you," she stammered. "You're..."

He was shaking a little himself in reaction to what had nearly happened. Adrenaline and fear coursed through him, pumping his blood fast and hard through his veins. "You know who I am. You just said my name," he pointed out. "And I damn well know who you are. So let's cut the bullshit. We don't have time for it. We need to get the hell out of here!"

She expelled a ragged sigh of resignation, as if she had finally given up trying to deny her true identity. Her palms patted his chest as if checking for bullet holes. "You didn't get shot?"

"No." But he suspected he had come uncomfortably close. If either of the gunmen, who were probably hired assassins, had been a better shot than he was, Josie would be in an entirely different situation right now.

As if she sensed that, she asked, "And those men?"

Brendan flinched with a pang of regret. But he had had no choice. If he hadn't shot the men, they would have killed him. And then they would have found Josie and the boy and killed them, too.

"They're not a threat. But the guy I left on the floor by your father's room could be."

Her breath audibly caught in a gasp of fear. "You left him there? He could hurt my father."

The assailant was in no condition to hurt anyone. Unless he'd regained consciousness...

"I don't think your father is their target," Brendan pointed out.

"They hurt him already," she said, reminding him of the reason the media mogul was in the hospital in the first place. Because he'd been attacked.

"That must have been just to lure you out of hiding." Someone had gone to a lot of trouble to track her down, and that someone was obviously very determined to do what Brendan had thought had been done almost four years ago. Kill Josie Jessup. If only he had had more time to interrogate the man downstairs, to find out who had hired him.

"They have no reason to hurt your father now," Brendan assured her before adding the obvious. "It's you they're after."

"And my son," she said, her voice cracking with emotion. "They were going to hurt him, too."

"Where is he?" he asked. His eyes had adjusted

to the darkness enough to see her before him now. "Where's my son?"

She shuddered again. "He's not your son."

"Stop," he impatiently advised her. "Just stop with the lies." She'd told him too many four years ago. "You need to get the boy and we need to get the hell out of here."

Because the bad men weren't the only threat.

Sirens wailed in the distance. Maybe just an ambulance on its way to the emergency room. Or maybe police cars on their way to secure a crime scene. He couldn't risk the latter. He couldn't be brought in for questioning or, worse, arrested. The local police wouldn't care that it had been self-defense; they were determined to arrest him for something. Anything. That was why Brendan had used the other fake orderly's gun. No bullets could be traced back to him. He'd wiped his prints off the weapon and left it on the roof.

"I'm not leaving with you," she said. "And neither is *my* son."

"You're in danger," he needlessly pointed out. "And you've put him in danger."

She sucked in a breath, either offended or feeling guilty. "And leaving with you would put us both in even more danger."

Now he drew in a sharp breath of pure offense. "If I wanted you gone, Josie, I could have just let those men shoot you."

"But they weren't going to shoot just me."

He flinched again at the thought of his child in so much danger. Reaching out, he grasped her shoulders. "Where is my son?" he repeated, resisting the urge to shake the truth out of her. "Someone wants you both dead. You can't let him out of your sight." And he couldn't let either of them out of his.

"I—I…"

"I won't hurt you," he assured her. "And I sure as hell won't hurt him."

Her head jerked in a sharp nod as if she believed him. He felt the motion more than saw it as her silky hair brushed his chin. She stepped back and turned around and then around again in a complete circle, as if trying to remember where she'd been.

"Where did you hide him?" he asked, hoping like hell that she had hidden him and hadn't just lost him.

"It was behind some exhaust pipes," she said. "I couldn't fit but he squeezed behind them. I—I just don't remember where they were."

"What's his name?"

She hesitated a moment before replying, as if his knowing his name would make the boy more real for Brendan. "CJ."

Maybe she was right—knowing the boy's name did make him more real to Brendan. His heart pounded and his pulse raced as he reeled from all the sudden realizations. He had a son. He was a father. He was continuing the "family" of which *he* had never wanted to be part.

"CJ," he repeated, then raised his voice and shouted, "CJ!"

"Shh." Josie cautioned him.

"He might not hear me if I don't yell," he pointed out. And Brendan needed to see his boy, to assure himself that his child was real and that he was all right.

"He won't come out if he hears *you,*" she explained. "He thinks you're a bad man."

Brendan flinched. It didn't matter that everyone else thought so; he didn't want his son to believe the lie, too.

"Is that what you told him?" he asked. It must have been what she'd believed all these years, because no matter how determined a reporter she'd been, she hadn't learned the truth about him.

"It's what you showed him," she said, "when you grabbed me by the elevator."

Dread and regret clenched his stomach muscles. His own son was afraid of him. How would he ever get close to the boy, ever form a relationship with him, if the kid feared him?

He flashed back so many years ago to his own heart pounding hard with fear as he cowered from his father, from the boom of his harsh voice and the sting of his big hand. Brendan hadn't just feared Dennis O'Hannigan. He'd been terrified of the man. But then so had everyone else.

"I'll be quiet," he whispered his promise. "You find him."

She called for the boy, her voice rising higher with panic each time she said his name. "CJ? CJ?" Then she sucked in a breath and her voice was steadier as she yelled, in a mother's no-nonsense tone, what must have been his full name, "Charles Jesse Brandt!"

Brandt? The boy's last name should have been O'Hannigan. But maybe it was better that it wasn't. Being an O'Hannigan carried with it so many dangers.

But then danger had found the boy no matter what his mother called him. CJ didn't respond to that maternal command only the rare child dared to disobey. Brendan certainly never would have disobeyed.

Panic clutched at his chest as worst-case scenarios began to play out in his mind. He had seen so many horrible things in his life that the possibilities kept coming. Had the man from the sixth floor somehow joined them on the roof without Brendan noticing? Had he found the boy already?

Another scenario played through his head, of Josie lying to him again. Still. Had she hidden the child and told him not to come out for Brendan? She'd hidden his son from him for three years—a few more minutes weren't going to bother her.

"Where is he?" he asked, shoving his hands in his pockets so that he wouldn't reach for her again. He had already frightened her, which was probably why she'd hidden their son from him.

She shook her head. "I don't know." The panic was in her voice, too.

Brendan almost preferred to think that she was lying to him and knew where the boy was, having made certain he was safe.

Her hand slapped against a metal pipe. "I thought he was behind here. CJ! CJ!"

"Then why isn't he coming out?" Brendan had stayed quiet and now kept his voice to a whisper despite the panic clutching at him.

"No, it can't be…" she murmured, her voice cracking with fear and dread.

"What?" He demanded to know the thought that occurred to her, that had her trembling now with fear.

"He's at the edge of the roof," she said. "He told me there was a short wall behind him. I—I told him not to go over it…"

Because there would have been nothing but the ground, twenty stories below, on the other side. If the boy was still on the roof with them, he would answer his mother. Even if he heard Brendan, he would come out to protect her, as he did before.

Oh, God!

Had Brendan lost his son only moments after finally finding him?

Chapter Five

Tears stung Josie's eyes, blinding her even more than the darkness. And sobs clogged her throat, choking her. She had been trying to protect her son, but she'd put him in more danger. She clawed at the pipes, trying to force them apart, trying to force her way back to where her son had been last.

"CJ! CJ!" she cried, her voice cracking with fear she could no longer contain.

She hadn't made sacrifices only to protect her father; she had made them to protect her baby, too. If she hadn't learned she was pregnant, she wouldn't have agreed to let her father hire bodyguards after the first attempt on her life—a cut brake line. And if she hadn't realized that no one could keep them truly safe, she wouldn't have agreed to fake her death and disappear.

Everything she'd done, she'd done for her son. Maybe that was why she'd brought him to see her father—not just so the two could finally meet, but so that her father would understand why she'd hurt him so badly. As a parent himself, he would have to understand and forgive her.

"CJ…" The tears overtook her now.

"Shh," a deep voice murmured, and a strong hand grasped her shoulder.

But the man didn't offer comfort.

"Shh," he said again, as a command. And his hand squeezed. "Listen."

Since Brendan was alive, she had just assumed that the men who'd wanted to kill her and CJ were not. But maybe he had just scared them off. And now they had returned. Or maybe that other gunman, the one he'd left near her father's room, had joined them on the roof.

She sucked in a breath, trying to calm herself. But if her child was truly gone, there would be no calming her—not even if the men had come back for them. They would need their guns—to defend themselves from her attack. This was their fault because they'd forced her to hide her son to protect him. But it wasn't their fault that she hadn't hidden him in a safe spot.

That was all on her.

"Shh," Brendan said again.

And she managed to control her sobs. But she heard their echo—coming softly from behind the metal pipes.

"CJ?" He wasn't gone. But why hadn't he come out? "Are you hurt?"

Perhaps there were more dangers behind the pipes than just that short wall separating him from a big fall. Maybe the pipes were hot. Or sharp.

"Listen," Brendan advised again.

The sobs were soft but strong and steady, not broken with pain, not weak with sickness. He was scared. Her little boy was too scared to come out, even for his mother.

"Tell him I'm not going to hurt him," Brendan said, his voice low but gruff. "Or you."

She nearly snorted in derision of his claim. When

he'd realized she had been working on a story about his father's murder, he'd been furious with her. Too furious to let her explain that even though the story was why she'd sought him out, she had really fallen in love with him.

Despite his difficult life, losing his mother, running away at fifteen, he'd seemed such a charming, loving man that she'd thought he might have fallen for her, too. But then his anger had showed another side of his personality, one dangerously similar to his merciless and vengeful father.

As if he'd heard the snort she'd suppressed, he insisted, "I'm not going to hurt either of you."

"Did you hear him, CJ?" she asked. "You don't have to be afraid." Then she drew in another breath to brace herself to lie to her son. "Mr. O'Hannigan is not a bad man."

She had actually been foolish enough to believe that once, to think that he was not necessarily his father's son. She'd thought that given all the years he'd spent away from the old man, he might have grown up differently. Honorably. That was why she'd fallen for him.

But when he'd learned she had actually been working on a story...

He hadn't been her charming lover. He had been cold and furious. But he hadn't been *only* furious. If he'd cut her brake line, he'd been vengeful, too. But she hadn't really meant anything to him then; she had been only a lover who'd betrayed him. Now he knew she was the mother of his child.

"He saved us from the bad men, CJ. The bad men are gone now." She turned back toward Brendan. He was just a dark shadow to her, but she discerned that his head jerked in a sharp nod.

She pushed her hand between the pipes, but no pudgy fingers caught hers. "CJ, you can come out now. It's safe."

She wasn't sure about that, but her son would be safer with her than standing just a short wall away from a long fall.

"It is safe." Brendan spoke now, his voice a low growl for her ears only. "But it may not stay that way. We need to get out of here before more *bad* men show up."

She shivered, either over his warning or his warm breath blowing in her ear and along her neck. Memories rushed back, of his breath on her neck before his lips touched her skin, skimming down her throat. His tongue flicking over her pulse before his mouth moved farther down her body...

Her pulse pounded faster, and she trembled. Then she forced the memories back, relegating them to where they belonged as she'd done so many times before. If she hadn't been able to keep the past in the past, she wouldn't have survived the past four years.

"CJ, why won't you come out?" she asked.

The boy sniffed hard, sucking up his tears and his snot. Josie flinched but resisted the urge to admonish him and was grateful she had done so when he finally spoke. "Cuz I—I was bad."

"No," Josie began, but another, deeper voice overwhelmed hers.

"No, son," Brendan said.

Josie gasped at his brazenness in addressing her child as his. Technically, biologically, it was true. But CJ didn't know that. And she never wanted him to learn the truth of his parentage. She never wanted him to know that he was one of *those* O'Hannigans.

"You weren't bad," Brendan continued. "You were very brave to protect your mother. You're a very good kid."

The boy sniffled again and released a shuddery breath.

"Now you have to be brave again," Brendan said. "And come out. There might be more bad men and we have to leave before they can be mean to your mother."

"You—you were mean to Mommy," CJ said. Her son was too smart to be as easily fooled by Brendan's charm as she had been. And as if compelled to protect her again, the little boy wriggled out from behind the pipes. But instead of confronting Brendan as he had inside the hospital, he ducked behind Josie's legs.

Brendan dropped to his haunches as if trying to meet the child's eyes even though it was so dark. "I shouldn't have been mean to her," he said. "And I'm sorry that I was. I thought she was someone else." His soft tone hardened. "Someone who lied to me, tricked me and then stole from me."

Josie shuddered at his implacable tone. He had saved her from the gunmen, but he hadn't forgotten her betrayal. Over the years it had apparently even been exaggerated in his mind, because she had never stolen anything from him. Judging by the anger he barely controlled, it seemed as if he would never forgive her.

"I don't like it when people lie to me," Brendan said. "But I would never hurt anyone."

"Who's lying now?" she murmured.

"Unless I had to in order to protect someone else," he clarified. "I will protect you and your mommy."

"I will p-tect Mommy," CJ said, obviously unwilling to share her with anyone else. But then, he'd never had to before. He had been the most important person—the only person, really—in her life since the day he was born.

Josie turned and lifted him in her arms. And she finally understood why he'd been so reluctant to come out of his hiding place. He was embarrassed, because his jeans were wet. Her little boy, who'd never had an accident since being potty-trained almost a year ago, had been so scared that he'd had one now. She clutched him close and whispered in his ear. "It's okay."

Brendan must have taken her words as acceptance. He slipped his arm around her shoulders. Despite the warmth of his body, she shivered in reaction to his closeness. Then he ushered her and CJ toward the elevator. He must have jammed the doors open, because it waited for them, light spilling from it onto the rooftop.

As she noticed that the armed men were gone, fear clutched at her. Brendan must not have injured them badly enough to stop them. They could be lurking in the shadows, ready to fire again. She covered CJ's face with her hand and leaned into Brendan, grateful for his size and his strength.

But then as they crossed the roof to the open doors, she noticed blood spattered across the asphalt and then smeared in two thick trails. Brendan had dragged away the bodies. Maybe he'd done it to spare their son from seeing death. Or maybe he'd done it to hide the evidence of the crime.

It hadn't actually been a crime though. It had been self-defense. And to protect her and their son. If she believed him...

But could she believe him? No matter what his motives were this time, the man was a killer. She didn't need to see the actual bodies to know that the men were dead. Her instincts were telling her that she shouldn't trust him. And she damn well shouldn't trust him with their son.

BRENDAN HELD HIS son. For the first time. But instead of a fragile infant, the boy was wriggly and surprisingly strong as he struggled in his grasp. He had taken him from Josie's arms, knowing that was the only way to keep her from running. She cared more about their son's safety than her own.

Maybe she really wasn't the woman he'd once known. Josie Jessup had been a spoiled princess, obviously uncaring of whom she hurt with her exposés and her actions. She had never run a story on Brendan though—she'd just run.

Brendan wouldn't let that happen again. So he held his son even though she reached for him, her arms outstretched. And the boy wriggled, trying to escape Brendan's grasp.

"Come on," he said to both of them. "We need to move quickly."

"I—I can run fast," CJ assured him.

Not fast enough to outrun bullets. Brendan couldn't be certain that the guy from the sixth floor hadn't regained consciousness and set up an ambush somewhere. He couldn't risk going through the hospital, so he pressed the garage express button on the elevator panel. It wouldn't stop on any other floors now. It would take them directly from the roof to the parking level in the basement.

"I'm sure you can run fast," Brendan said. "But we all have to stay together from now on to make sure we stay safe from the bad men."

But the little boy stopped struggling and stared up

at him, his blue-green eyes narrowed as if he was trying to see inside Brendan—to see if he was a bad man, too. He hoped like hell the kid couldn't really see inside his soul.

It was a dark, dark place. It had been even darker when he'd thought Josie had been murdered. He had thought that she'd been killed because of him—because she'd gotten too close, because she'd discovered something that he should have.

From the other stories she'd done, he knew she was a good reporter. Too good. So good that she could have made enemies of her own, though.

At first he hadn't thought this attack on her had anything to do with him. After all, he hadn't even known she was alive. And he'd certainly had no idea he had a child.

But maybe one of *his* enemies had discovered she was alive. She stared up at him with the same intensity of their son, her eyes just a lighter, smokier green. No matter how much her appearance had been altered and what she'd claimed before, she was definitely Josie Jessup. And whoever had discovered she was really alive knew what Brendan hadn't realized until he heard of her death—that he'd fallen for her. Despite her lies. Despite her betrayal.

He had fallen in love with her, with her energy and her quick wit and her passion. And he'd spent more than three years mourning her. Someone might have wanted to make certain that his mourning never ended.

Josie shook her head, rejecting his protection. "I think we'll be safer on our own."

She didn't trust him. Given his reputation, or at least the reputation of his family, he didn't necessarily blame her. But then she should have known him better. During those short months they'd spent together before her "death," he had let her get close. He may not have told her the truth about himself, but he'd shown her that he wasn't the man others thought he was. He wasn't his father.

He wasn't cruel and indifferent. "If I'd left you alone on the roof…"

SHE AND CJ would already be dead. She shuddered in revulsion at the horrible thought. She could not deny that Brendan O'Hannigan had saved their lives. But she was too scared to thank him and too smart to trust him.

Despite her inner voice warning her to be careful, she had thought only of her father when she'd risked coming to the hospital. She hadn't considered that after spending more than three years in hiding someone might still want to kill her. She hadn't considered that someone could have learned that she was still alive. "I was caught off guard."

Brendan stared down at the boy he held in his arms. "I can relate."

He had seemed shocked, not only to find her alive but also to realize that he was a father. Given that they had exactly the same eyes and facial features, Brendan had instantly recognized the child as his. There had been no point for her to continue denying what it wouldn't require a DNA test to prove.

"Are you usually on guard?" he asked her.

"Yes." But when she'd learned of the assault on her father, she had dropped her guard. And it had nearly cost her everything. She couldn't take any more risks. And trusting Brendan would be the greatest risk of all. "I won't make that mistake again."

"No," he said, as if he agreed with her. Or supported her. But then he added, "I won't let you."

And she tensed. She lifted her arms again and clasped her hands on her son's shoulders. After nearly losing him on the rooftop, she should have held him so tightly that he would never get away. But he'd started wriggling in the elevator, and she'd loosened her grip just enough that Brendan had been able to easily pluck him from her.

A chill chased down her spine as she worried that he would take her son from her just that easily. And permanently.

Josie's stomach rose as the elevator descended to the basement. Panic filled her throat, choking her. Then the bell dinged, signaling that they had reached their destination. They had gone from one extreme to another, one danger to another.

"We'll take my car," Brendan said as the doors slowly began to slide open.

We. He didn't intend to take her son and leave her alone, or as he'd left the men on the rooftop. Dead. But she and her son couldn't leave with him, either. She shook her head.

"We don't have time to argue right now," he said, his deep voice gruff with impatience. "We need to get out of here."

"Do you have a car seat?" she asked. She had posed the question to thwart him, thinking she already knew the answer. But she didn't. As closely as she followed the news, she hadn't heard or read anything about Brendan O'Hannigan's personal life. Only about his business. Or his *alleged* business.

He'd kept his personal life far more private than his professional one. But she had been gone for more than three years. He could have met someone else. Could even have had another child, one he'd known about, one with whom he lived.

He clenched his jaw and shook his head.

"CJ is too little to ride without a car seat."

"I'm not little!" her son heartily protested, as he twisted even more forcefully in Brendan's grasp. Her hands slipped from his squirming shoulders. "I'm big!"

If CJ had been struggling like that in her arms, she would have lost him, and just as the doors opened fully. And he might have run off to hide again.

But Brendan held him firmly, but not so tightly that he hurt the boy. With his low pain threshold, her son would have been squealing if he'd felt the least bit of discomfort.

"You are big," Josie assured him. "But the law says you're not big enough to ride without your car seat."

Arching a brow, she turned toward Brendan. "You don't want to break the law, do you?"

A muscle twitched along his clenched jaw. He shook his head but then clarified, "I don't want to risk CJ's safety."

But she had no illusions that if not for their son, he would have no qualms about breaking the law. She had no illusions about Brendan O'Hannigan anymore.

But she once had. She'd begun to believe that his inheriting his father's legacy had forced him into a life he wouldn't have chosen, one he'd actually run from when he was a kid. She'd thought he was better than that life, that he was a good man.

What a fool she'd been.

"Where's your car?" he asked as he carried their son from the elevator.

She hurried after them, glancing at the cement pillars, looking at the signs.

"What letter, Mommy?" CJ asked. He'd been sleeping when she'd parked their small SUV, so he didn't know. She could lie and he wouldn't contradict her as he had earlier.

But lying about the parking level would only delay the inevitable. She wasn't going to get CJ away from his father without a struggle, one that might hurt her son. Or at least scare him. And the little boy had already been frightened enough to last him a lifetime.

"A," she replied.

CJ pointed a finger at the sign. "That's this one."

"What kind of car?" Brendan asked.

"A—a white Ford Escape," she murmured.

"And the plate?"

She shook her head and pointed toward where the rear bumper protruded beyond two bigger sport utility vehicles parked on either side of it. "It's right there."

Because CJ had been sleeping, she'd made certain to park close to the elevators so she wouldn't have far to carry him. As he said, he was a big boy—at least big enough that carrying him too far or for too long strained her arms and her back.

She shoved her hand in her jeans pocket to retrieve the keys. She'd locked her purse inside the vehicle to protect her new identity just in case anyone recognized her inside the hospital. She was grateful she'd taken the precaution. But if she'd had her cell phone and her can of mace, maybe she wouldn't have needed Brendan to come to her rescue.

Lifting the key fob, she pressed the unlock button. The lights flashed and the horn beeped. But then another sound drowned out that beep as gunshots rang out. The echo made it impossible to tell from which direction the shots were coming.

But she didn't need to know where they were coming from to know where they were aimed—at her. Bullets whizzed past her head, stirring her hair.

A strong hand clasped her shoulder, pushing her down so forcefully that she dropped to the ground. Her knees struck the cement so hard that she involuntarily cried out in pain.

A cry echoed hers—CJ's. He hadn't fallen; he was still clasped tightly in Brendan's arms. But one of those flying bullets could have struck him.

Now she couldn't cry. She couldn't move. She could only stay on the ground, frozen with terror and dread that she had failed her son once again.

Chapter Six

Vivid curses reverberated inside Brendan's head, echoing the cries of the woman and the child. Those cries had to be of fear—just fear. He'd made certain that they wouldn't be hit, keeping them low as the shots rang out. If only he'd had backup waiting…

But just as he had taken on the gunmen inside the hospital, he also had to confront this one alone—while trying to protect people he hadn't even known were alive until tonight. So he didn't utter those curses echoing inside his head, not only because of his son but also because he didn't have time.

He'd taken the gun off the guy he'd left alive. But that didn't mean the man hadn't had another one on him, as Brendan always did. Or maybe if he'd come down to ambush them in the garage he'd retrieved a weapon from his vehicle.

Where the hell were the shots coming from? Since they ricocheted off the cement floor and ceiling and pillars, he couldn't tell. So he couldn't fire back—even if he'd had a free hand to grab one of his concealed weapons.

His hands were full, one clasping his son tightly to his chest while his other wrapped around Josie's arm.

He lifted her from the ground and tugged her toward the car she'd unlocked. Thankfully, it was next to two bigger SUVs that provided some cover as he ushered them between the vehicles.

"Do you still have the keys?" he asked.

Josie stared at him wide-eyed, as if too scared to comprehend what he was saying, or maybe the loud gunshots echoing throughout the parking structure had deafened her. Or she was just in shock.

Brendan leaned closer to her, his lips nearly brushing her ear as her hair tickled his cheek. Then he spoke louder. "Keys?"

She glanced down at her hand. A ring of keys dangled from her trembling fingers.

He released her arm to grab the keys from her. Then, with the keys jamming into his palm, he pulled open the back door and thrust her inside the vehicle.

"Stay low," he said, handing their son to her. As he slammed the door shut behind them, a bullet hit the rear bumper. The other vehicles offered no protection if the shooter was behind them now.

Brendan let a curse slip out of his lips. Then he quickly pulled open the driver's door. As he slid behind the steering wheel, he glanced into the rearview mirror. He couldn't see anyone in the backseat. Josie had taken his advice and stayed low.

But he noticed someone else. A dark shadow moved between cars parked on the other side of the garage, rushing toward Josie's SUV. In the dim lighting, he couldn't see the guy's face, couldn't tell if this was the supposed orderly from the sixth floor. He couldn't risk the guy getting close enough for Brendan to recognize him.

He shoved the keys in the ignition. As soon as

the motor turned over, he reversed. He would have slammed into the cars behind them, would have tried to crush the shooter. But Josie and the boy were not buckled in, so he couldn't risk their being tossed around the vehicle.

And Brendan couldn't risk the gunman getting close enough to take more shots. If these guys were all hired professionals, they were bound to get an accurate shot. So he shifted into Drive and pressed his foot down on the accelerator. If only he could reach for one of his weapons and shoot back at the shadow running after them…

But he needed both hands on the wheel, needed to carefully careen around the sharp curves so he didn't hit a concrete pillar, or fling Josie and his son out a window. He had to make sure that he didn't kill them while he tried so desperately to save them.

Josie didn't know what would kill them first: the gunshots or a car accident. Since Brendan was driving so fast, he must have outdistanced the gunman so no bullets could fly through the back window and strike CJ. She quickly strapped him into his booster seat. As short as he was, his head was still beneath the headrest.

"Stay down," Brendan warned her from the front seat as he swerved around more sharp corners and headed up toward the street level and the exit. "There could be more—"

Hired killers? That was probably what he'd intended to say before stopping himself for their son's sake, not wanting to scare the boy.

"Bad men?" she asked. She hadn't expected any of them or she never would have brought her son to the hospital. She wouldn't have put him at risk. How the hell had someone found out she was alive?

He had acted surprised. Had he really not known until tonight?

She had so many questions, but asking Brendan would have been a waste of time. He had never told her anything she'd wanted to know before. And she wasn't certain that he would actually have any answers this time. If he really hadn't known she was alive, he would have no idea who was trying to kill her.

She needed to talk to Charlotte.

Leaning forward, she reached under the driver's seat and tugged out the purse she'd stashed there earlier. She hadn't left only her identification inside but also her cell phones. Her personal phone and that special cell used only to call her handler. But Josie couldn't make that confidential call, not with Brendan in the vehicle.

"What are you doing?" he asked, with a quick glance in the rearview mirror. He probably couldn't see her, but he'd felt it when she'd reached under his seat. Was the man aware of everything going on around him? Given his life and his enemies, he probably had to be—or *he* wouldn't be alive still.

"Getting my purse," she said.

"Do you have a weapon in it?" he asked.

"Why?" Did he want her to use it or was he worried that she would? She reached inside the bag and wrapped her fingers around the can of mace. But even if he wasn't driving so fast, she couldn't have risked spraying it and hurting her son.

His gaze went to the rearview mirror again. "Never mind. I think we lost him," he said. But he didn't stop at the guard shack for the parking garage. Instead he crashed the SUV right through the gate.

CJ cried, and Josie turned to him with concern. But his cry was actually a squeal as his teal-blue eyes twinkled with excitement. What had happened to her timid son?

She leaned over the console between the seats. "Be careful."

"Are you all right?" he asked. "And CJ?"

"We're both fine. But is the car all right?" she asked. One of the headlamps wobbled, bouncing the beam of light around the street. "I need to be able to drive it home."

But first she had to get rid of Brendan.

"You can't go home," he told her. "The gunman was coming up behind the vehicle. He could have gotten your plate and pulled up your registration online. He could already know where you live."

She didn't know what would be worse: the gunman knowing where she lived or Brendan knowing. But she wouldn't need to worry about either scenario. Charlotte had made certain of that. "The vehicle isn't registered to me."

JJ Brandt was only one of the identities the U.S. marshal had set up for her. In case one of those identities was compromised, she could assume a new one. But for nearly four years, she had never come close to being recognized. Until tonight, when no one had been fooled by her new appearance or her new name.

Thanks to Brendan's interference, JJ Brandt hadn't died tonight. Literally. But she would have to die figuratively since Brendan might have learned that name. And she would have to assume one of the other identities.

But she couldn't do anything until she figured out how to get rid of him. Maybe she needed to ask him how to do that. He was the one around whom people tended to disappear.

First her.

But according to the articles she'd read, there had been others. Some members of his "family" and some of his business rivals had disappeared over the past four years. No bodies had been found, so no charges had been brought against him. But the speculation was that he was responsible for those disappearances.

She'd believed he was responsible for hers, too, blaming him for those attempts on her life that had driven her into hiding. Since he'd saved her on the roof and again in the garage, she wanted to believe she'd been wrong about him.

But what if she'd been right? Then she'd gotten into a vehicle with a killer. Was she about to go away for good?

THE FARTHER THEY traveled from the hospital, the quieter it was. No gunshots. No sirens. He'd made certain to drive away from the emergency entrance so that he wouldn't cross paths with ambulances or, worse yet, police cars. It wasn't quiet only outside, but it was eerily silent inside the vehicle, too.

Brendan glanced at the rearview mirror, his gaze going first to his son. He still couldn't believe he had a child; he was a *father*.

The boy slept, his red curls matted against the side pad of his booster seat. Drool trickled from the corner of his slightly open mouth. How had he fallen asleep so easily after so much excitement?

Adrenaline still coursed through Brendan's veins, making his pulse race and his heart pound. But maybe it wasn't just because of the gunfire and the discovery that Josie was alive and had given birth to his baby.

Maybe it was because of her. She was so close to

him that he could feel the warmth of her body. Or maybe that was just the heat of his own attraction to her. She didn't look exactly the same, but she made him feel the same. Just as before, she *made* him feel when he didn't want to feel anymore.

She leaned over the console, her shoulder brushing against his as she studied the route he was taking. Did she recognize it? She'd taken it several times over those few months they had gone out. But then that was nearly four years ago.

Four years in which she'd been living another life and apparently not alone. And not with only their son, either.

"This isn't your vehicle?" Brendan asked, unable to hold back the question any longer. It had been nagging at him since she'd said the plate wasn't registered to her.

"What?" she asked.

"You borrowed it from someone else?" Or had she taken it from a driveway they shared? Was she living with someone? A boyfriend? A husband?

And what would that man be to CJ? His *uncle?* Stepfather? Or did he just have CJ call him *Daddy?*

Had another man claimed Brendan's son as his?

"Borrowed what?" she asked, her voice sounding distracted as if she were as weary as their son. Or maybe she was wary. Fearful of telling him too much about her new life for fear that he would track her down.

"This vehicle. You borrowed it?" Maybe that was the real reason she had worried about him wrecking it—it would make someone else angry with her.

"No," she said. "It's mine."

Had someone given it to her? Gifted her a vehicle? It might have seemed extravagant to the man. But to

Stanley Jessup's daughter? She was able to buy herself a fleet of luxury vehicles on her weekly allowance.

"But it's not registered to your name?" he asked. "To your address?"

"No, it's not," she said. And her guard was back up.

His jealousy was gone. The vehicle wasn't a gift; it was registered under someone else's name and address to protect her, to prevent someone running her plates and finding where she and her son were living.

"You do usually have your guard up," he observed. "You are very careful."

"Until tonight," she murmured regretfully. "I never should have come here."

"No," he agreed. "Not if you wanted to stay in hiding."

"I *have* to stay in hiding."

"Why?" he asked.

She gasped. "I think, after tonight, it would be quite obvious why I had to…" Her voice cracked, but she cleared her throat and added, "Disappear."

Brendan nodded in sudden realization of where she had been for almost four years. "You've been in witness protection."

Her silence gave him the answer that he should have come to long ago. He was painfully familiar with witness protection. But he couldn't tell her that. Her identity might have changed, but he suspected at heart she was still a reporter. He couldn't tell her anything without the risk of it showing up in one of her father's papers or on one of his news programs.

So he kept asking the questions. "Why were you put in witness protection?"

What had she seen? What did she know? Maybe

she'd learned, in those few short months, more than he'd realized. More than he had learned in four years.

"What did you witness?" he asked.

She shrugged and her shoulder bumped against his. "Nothing that I was aware of. Nothing I could testify about."

"Then why would the marshals put you in *witness* protection?"

Her breath shuddered out, caressing his cheek. "Because someone tried to kill me."

"Was it like tonight?" he asked.

She snorted derisively. "You don't know?"

So she assumed he would know how someone had tried to kill her. But he didn't. "You were shot at back then?"

"No," she said. "The attempts were more subtle than that. A cut brake line on my car." She had driven a little sports car—too fast and too recklessly. He remembered the report of her accident. At the time he had figured her driving had caused it. She was lucky that the accident hadn't killed her. "And then there was the explosion."

"That was subtle," he scoffed. The explosion had destroyed the house she'd been staying in, as well as her "remains," so that she'd only been identifiable by DNA. "It wasn't just a ploy the marshals used to put you into witness protection?"

She shook her head and now her hair brushed his cheek. His skin tingled and heated in reaction to her maddening closeness. He should have told her to sit back and buckle up next to their son. Or pulled her over the console into the passenger's seat.

But she was closer where she was, so he said nothing.

"No," Josie replied. "Someone found the supposedly *safe* house where I was staying after the cut brake line and set the bomb to try again to kill me."

No wonder she'd gone into protection again. Faking her death might have been the only way to keep her alive. But he might have come up with another way… if she'd told him about the attempts.

But they hadn't been talking then. He'd been too furious with her when he'd discovered that she'd been duping him—only getting close for a damn exposé for her father's media organizations. Once Brendan had figured out her pen name, he'd found the stories she'd done. No one had been safe around her, not even her classmates when she'd been at boarding school and later at college.

None of her friends had been safe from her, either. Maybe that was why she'd had few when they'd met. Maybe that was why it had been so easy for her to leave everyone behind.

Including him.

Except her father. That was why she'd come to the hospital after he'd been assaulted. Perhaps they hadn't actually severed contact, as she had with Brendan— never even letting him know he'd become a father.

She probably didn't know the identity of her would-be killer or she wouldn't have had to stay in hiding all this time. But he asked anyway. "Who do you think was trying to kill you?"

She answered without hesitation and with complete certainty, "You."

Chapter Seven

Maybe Josie was as tired as her son was. Why else would she have made such an admission? Moreover, why else would she have let him drive her here—of all places?

She should have recognized the route, since her gaze had never left the road as he'd driven them away from the hospital. She had driven here so many times over those months when they had been seeing each other. She'd preferred going to his place, hoping that she would find something or overhear something the police didn't know that could have led her to a break in his father's murder investigation.

And she hadn't wanted him to find anything at her apartment that would have revealed that she was so much more than just the empty-headed heiress so many others had thought she was. Things like her journalism awards or her diploma or the scrapbook of articles she'd published under her pseudonym.

But it didn't matter that he had never found any of those things. Somehow he'd learned the truth about who she was anyway. And after the ferocious fight they'd had, the attempts on her life had begun.

"How could you think I would have tried to kill

you?" he asked, his voice a rasp in the eerie silence of the vehicle. Even CJ wasn't making any sounds as he slept so deeply and quietly.

Brendan had pulled the SUV through the wrought-iron gates of the O'Hannigan estate, but they had yet to open the car doors. They remained sealed in that tomblike silence he'd finally broken with his question.

"How could I *not* think it was you?" she asked, keeping her voice to a low whisper so that she didn't wake her son. He didn't need to know that tonight wasn't the first time a bad man had tried to hurt his mommy. Even the authorities had suspected Brendan O'Hannigan was responsible. That was why they'd offered her protection—to keep her alive to testify against him once they found evidence that he'd been behind the attempts. "Who else would want me dead?"

He turned toward her, and since she still leaned over the console, he was close. His face was just a breath away from hers. And his eyes—the same rare blue-green as her son's—were narrowed, his brow furrowed with confusion as he stared at her. "Why would *I* want you dead?"

"I lied to you. I tricked you," she said, although she doubted he needed any reminders. And given how angry he'd been with her, she shouldn't have reminded him, shouldn't have brought back all his rage and vengeance. He might forget that she was the mother of his son. Of course he had earlier mentioned those things to their son. He'd included stealing, too, although she'd stolen nothing from him but perhaps his trust.

Despite how angry he'd been, Brendan literally shrugged off her offenses, as if they were of no consequence to him. His broad shoulder rubbed against hers, making her skin tingle even beneath her sweater and jacket. "I've been lied to and tricked before," he said.

She doubted that many people would have been brave enough to take on Dennis O'Hannigan's son— the man that many people claimed was a chip off the block of evil. She still couldn't believe that she had summoned the courage. But then she'd been a different woman four years ago. She'd been an adrenaline junkie who had gotten high on the rush of getting the story. The more information she had discovered the more excited she had become. She hadn't been only brave—she'd been fearless.

Then she had become a mother, and she had learned what fear was. Now she was always afraid, afraid that her son would get sick or hurt or scared. Or that whoever had tried to kill her would track them down and hurt him.

And tonight that fear, her deepest, darkest fear, had been realized. She shuddered, chilled by the thought. But the air had grown cold inside the car now that Brendan had shut off the engine. His heavily muscled body was close and warm, but the look on his ridiculously handsome face was cold. Even colder than the air.

"And," he continued, "I never killed any of those people."

With a flash of that old fearlessness, she scoffed, "Never?" All the articles about Brendan O'Hannigan alleged otherwise. "That's not what I've heard."

"You, of all people, should know better than to believe everything you hear or read," he advised her.

Growing up the daughter of a media magnate, she'd heard the press disparaged more than she'd heard fairy tales. Fairy tales. What was a bigger lie than a fairy tale? Than a promise of happily-ever-after?

"If it's coming from a credible source, which all of my father's news outlets are, then you should believe the story," she said.

He snorted. "What makes a source *credible?*"

As the daughter of a newsman, she'd grown up instinctively knowing what a good source was. "An insider. Someone close to the story."

"An eyewitness?" He was the one scoffing now.

She doubted anyone had witnessed him committing any crime and lived to testify. She shivered again and glanced at their son. She shouldn't have put his life in the hands of a killer. But the gunman in the garage had given her no choice. Neither had Brendan.

"Even grand juries rarely issue an indictment on eyewitness testimony," he pointed out, as if familiar with the legal process. "They need evidence to bring charges."

Had he personally been brought before a grand jury? Or was he just familiar with the process from all the times district attorneys had tried to indict his father? But she knew better than to ask the questions that naturally came to her. He had never answered any of her questions before.

But he kept asking his own inquiries. "Is there any evidence that I'm a—" Brendan glanced beyond her, into the backseat where their son slept peacefully, angelically "—a bad man?"

She hadn't been able to find anything that might have proven his guilt. She'd looked hard for that evidence—not just for her story but also for herself. She'd wanted a reason not to give in to her attraction to him, a reason not to fall for him.

But when, as a journalist, she hadn't been able to come up with any cold, hard facts, she'd let herself, as a woman, fall in love with an incredibly charming and smart man. And then he'd learned the truth about her.

What was the truth about him?

BRENDAN WAITED, but she didn't answer him. Could she really believe that he was a killer? Could she really believe that he had tried to kill *her?*

Sure, he had been furious because she'd deceived him. But he'd only been so angry because he'd let himself fall for her. He'd let himself believe that she might have fallen for him, too, when she'd actually only been using him.

He wasn't the only one she'd used. There were the friends in boarding school she'd used as inside sources to get dirt on their famous parents. Then there was the Peterson kid in college with a violence and drug problem that the school had been willing to overlook to keep their star athlete. She'd used her friendship with the kid to blow the lid off that, too. Hell, her story had probably started all the subsequent exposés on college athletic programs. It had also caused the kid to kill himself.

"You really think that I'm the only one who might want you dead?" Josie Jessup had been many things but never naive.

She gasped as if shocked by his question. Or maybe offended. How the hell did she think he felt with her believing he was a killer?

He was tempted, as he'd been four years ago, to tell her the truth. But then he'd found out she was really a reporter after a story, and as mad as he'd been, he'd also been relieved that he hadn't told her anything that could have blown his assignment.

Hell, it wasn't just an assignment. It was a mission. Of justice.

She didn't care about that, though. She cared only about exposés and Pulitzers and ratings. And her father's approval.

But then maybe his mission of justice was all about his father, too. About finally getting his approval—postmortem.

"Who else would want me dead?" she asked.

"Whoever else might have found out that you wrote all those stories under the byline Jess Ley." It was a play on the name of her father, Stanley Jessup. Some people thought the old man had written the stories himself.

But Brendan had been with her the night the story on her college friend had won a national press award. And he'd seen the pride and guilt flash across her face. And, finally, he'd stopped playing a fool and really checked her out, and all his fears had been confirmed.

She sucked in a breath and that same odd mixture of pride and guilt flashed across her face. "I don't even know how you found out.…"

"You gave yourself away," he said. "And anyone close to you—close to those stories—would have figured out you'd written them, too."

She shook her head in denial, and her silky hair skimmed along her jaw and across his cheek. No matter how much she'd changed her appearance, she was still beautiful, still appealing.

He wanted to touch her hair. To touch her face…

But he doubted she would welcome the hands of the man she thought was her would-be killer. "If I wanted you dead, I wouldn't have helped you tonight," he pointed out.

She glanced back at their sleeping son. "You did it for him. You know what it's like to grow up without a mother."

So did she. That was something that had connected them, something they'd had in common in lives that had been so disparate. They'd understood each other intimately—emotionally and physically.

He shook his head, trying to throw off those memories and the connection with her that had him wanting her despite her lies and subterfuge.

"That was sloppy tonight and dangerous," he said, dispassionately critiquing the would-be assassins, "trying to carry off a hit in a hospital."

His father and his enemies would have been indicted long ago if they had operated their businesses as sloppily. Whoever had hired the assassins had not gotten their money's worth.

Neither had the U.S. Marshals. Like the local authorities, they must have been so desperate to pin something on him that they'd taken her word that he was behind the attempts on her life. They'd put her into protection and worried about finding evidence later. Like her, they had never come up with any. No reason to charge him.

If only they knew the truth...

But the people who knew it had been kept to a minimum—to protect his life and the lives of those around him. So it might not have been his fault that someone had tried to kill Josie, yet he felt responsible.

JOSIE REALIZED THAT he was right. Even if he hadn't been with her tonight, in the line of fire on the roof and in the garage, it was possible that he had nothing to do with the attempts on her life.

Brendan O'Hannigan was never sloppy.

If he was, there would have been evidence against him and charges brought before a grand jury that would have elicited an indictment. No. Brendan O'Hannigan was anything but sloppy. He was usually ruthlessly controlled—except in bed. With her caresses and her kisses, she had made him lose control.

And that one day that had her shivering in remembrance, she'd made him lose his temper. The media hadn't been wrong about her being spoiled. Her father had never so much as raised his voice to her. So Brendan's cold fury had frightened her.

If only it had killed her attraction to him, as he had tried to kill her. Not tonight, though. She believed he hadn't been behind the attempt at the hospital.

If he'd wanted her gone, he would have brought her someplace private. Someplace remote. Where no one could witness what he did to her.

Someplace like the O'Hannigan estate.

"You're cold," he said. As close as they were he must have felt her shiver. And the windows were also steaming up on the inside and beginning to ice on the outside. It was a cold spring, the temperature dropping low at night.

And it was late.

Too late?

"Let's go inside," he said.

It would be too late for her if she went inside the mansion with him. She still clutched her purse, her hand inside and still wrapped around her cell phone— the special one she used only to call Charlotte. But she released her grip on it.

It wouldn't help her against the immediate threat he posed. She didn't even know where Charlotte was, let alone if she could reach her in time to help.

"I'll get CJ," he offered as he opened the driver's door. But she hurried out the back door, stepping between him and their sleeping son.

"No," she said.

"He's getting cold out here."

Brendan tried to reach around her, but she pushed him back with her body, pressing it up against his. Her pulse leaped in reaction to his closeness.

"You can't bring him inside," she said, "not until you make sure it's safe."

He gestured toward the high wrought-iron fence encircling the estate. "The place is a fortress."

"You don't live here alone," she said.

"You really shouldn't believe everything you read," he said.

So obviously if there had been something in the news about a live-in girlfriend, it hadn't been from a credible source. Despite her fear of him, she felt a flash of relief.

"You don't take care of this place yourself," she pointed out. "You have live-in staff."

He nodded in agreement and leaned closer, trying to reach around her. "And I know and trust every one of them."

She clicked her tongue against her teeth in admonishment. "You should know that you can't trust anyone."

He stared at her and gave a sharp nod of agreement before stepping back. "You're right."

She held in a sigh of relief, especially as he continued to stare at her. Then he reached inside the open driver's door and pulled out the keys. Obviously she was the one he did not trust—not to drive off without him. He knew her too well.

"I'll check it out." He slid the keys into his suit pocket. "And come back for you."

With a soft click, she closed the back door. "I'll go with you."

As they headed up the brick walk toward the front door, she reached inside her bag for the can of mace. She would spray it at him and retrieve the keys while he was coughing and sputtering.

She could get away from him. She could protect her son and herself.

"Remember the first time you walked up this path with me?" Brendan asked, his deep voice a warm rasp in the cold.

She shivered as a tingle of attraction chased up her spine. Their fingers had been entwined that night. They had been holding hands since dinner at a candlelit restaurant.

"I teased you about playing the gentleman," he reminisced. "And you said that you were no gentleman because you just wanted to get me alone."

Her face heated as she remembered what a brazen flirt she'd been. But she'd acted that way only with him. And it hadn't been just for the story. It had been for the way his gorgeous eyes had twinkled with excitement and attraction. And it had been for the rush of her pulse.

Brendan chuckled but his voice was as cold as the night air. "You really just wanted to get inside."

That wasn't the situation tonight. Inside his house, with its thick brick walls and leaded-glass windows to hold in her screams, was the last place Josie wanted to be. Maybe he hadn't been a bad man four years ago, but he'd only just begun taking over his father's business then. Now that business was his. And he'd been leaving his own legacy of missing bodies.

"You just wanted to search my stuff," he angrily continued, "see what secrets you could find to shout out to the rest of the world through one of your father's publications."

"You're so bitter over my misleading you," she remarked. "Can't you see why I would think you're the one who wants me dead?"

He sighed and dragged out a ring of keys from his pants pocket. She recognized them because she'd tried so often to get them away from him—so she could make copies, so she could come and go at will in his house, business and offices.

"If you would realize why I am so bitter," he said, "you would also understand why the last thing I want is for you to be gone."

He turned away from the door and stared down at her, as he had that first night he'd brought her home with him. His pupils had swallowed the blue-green irises then, as they did now. "I wanted you with me that night…and all the nights that followed."

There was that charm that had given her hope that he was really a good man. That charm had distracted and disarmed her before.

But she hadn't had CJ to worry about and protect then. So now she kept her hand wrapped tightly around the can of mace. And when he lowered his head toward hers, she started to pull it from her purse.

But then his lips touched hers, brushing softly across them. And her breath caught as passion knocked her down as forcefully as he had earlier in the parking garage.

He had saved her tonight. He had saved her and her son. And reminding herself of that allowed her to kiss him back. For just a moment though…

Because he pulled away and turned back toward the door. And she did what she should have done as he'd lowered his head—she pulled out the can of mace and lifted it toward him.

Then she smelled it. The odor lay heavy on the cold air, drifting beneath the door of the house. She dragged in a deep breath to double-check.

Maybe she was just imagining it, as she had so often the past four years, waking in the middle of the night shaking with fear. She had to check the stove and the furnace and the water heater.

And though she never found a leak, she never squelched those fears. That this time no one would notice the bomb before it exploded.

This time the fire wouldn't eat an empty house. It would eat hers, with her and CJ trapped inside. But this wasn't her house.

It was Brendan's, and he was sliding his key into the lock. Would it be the lock clicking or the turning of the knob that would ignite the explosion?

She dropped the damn can and reached for him, screaming as her nightmare became a fiery reality.

Chapter Eight

Flames illuminated the night, licking high into the black sky. The boy was screaming. Despite the ringing in his ears, Brendan could hear him, and his heart clutched with sympathy for the toddler's fear.

He could hear the fire trucks, too, their sirens whining in the distance. Ambulances and police cars probably followed or led them—he couldn't tell the difference between the sirens.

Despite the slight shaking in his legs, he pressed harder on the accelerator, widening the distance between Josie's little white SUV and the fiery remains of the mansion where he'd grown up.

It had never been home, though. That was why he'd run away when he was fifteen and why he'd intended never to return. If not for feeling that he owed his father justice, he would have never come back.

"Are—are you sure you want to leave?" Josie stammered, wincing as if her own voice hurt her ears. She was in the front seat but leaning into the back this time, her hand squeezing one of their son's flailing fists. She'd been murmuring softly to the boy, trying to calm him down since they'd jumped back into the vehicle and taken off.

The poor kid had been through so much tonight, it was no wonder he'd gotten hysterical, especially over how violently he'd been awakened from his nap.

"Are you sure?" Josie prodded Brendan for an answer, as she always had.

He replied, this time with complete honesty, "I have no reason to stay."

"But your staff…"

Wouldn't have survived that explosion. Nothing would have. If he hadn't noticed the smell before he'd turned that key, if Josie hadn't clutched his arms…

They would have been right next to the house when a staff member inside, who must have noticed the key rattling in the door, had opened it for them and unknowing set off the bomb. Instead he and Josie had been running for the SUV, for their son, when the bomb exploded. The force of it had knocked them to the ground and rocked her vehicle.

"Are you all right?" he asked again.

She'd jumped right up and continued to run, not stopping until she'd reached their screaming son. The explosion had not only awakened but terrified him. Or maybe he felt the fear that had her trembling uncontrollably.

She jerked her chin in an impatient nod. "Yes, I—I'm okay."

"Maybe we should have stayed," he admitted. But his first instinct had been to get the hell away in case the bomber had hung around to finish the job if the explosion hadn't killed them.

While Brendan wished he could soothe his son's fears, his first priority was to keep the boy and his mother safe. And healthy. "We should have you checked out."

She shook her head. "Nobody can see me, in case they recognize me like you did. And those other men…" She shuddered, probably as she remembered the ordeal those men had put her and CJ through. "We can't go back to the hospital anyway."

"There are urgent-care facilities that are open all night," he reminded her. Maybe her new location wasn't near a big city and she'd forgotten the amenities and conveniences of one.

She shook her head. "But someone there might realize we were at this explosion…" The smell of smoke had permeated the car and probably her hair. "And they might call the police," she said. "Or the media."

He nearly grinned at the irony of her wanting to avoid the press.

"And it's not necessary," she said, dismissing his concerns. "I'm okay."

He glanced toward the backseat. CJ's screams had subsided to hiccups and sniffles. Brendan's heart ached with the boy's pain and fear. "What about our son?"

"He's scared," Josie explained. And from the way she kept trembling, the little boy wasn't the only one.

"It's okay," she assured the child, and perhaps she was assuring herself, too. "We're getting far away from the fire."

Not so far that the glow of the fire wasn't still visible in the rearview mirror, along with the billows of black smoke darkening the sky even more.

"It won't hurt us," she said. "It won't hurt us…."

"We're going someplace very safe," Brendan said, "where no bad men can find us."

He shouldn't have brought them back to the mansion. But the place was usually like a fortress, so he hadn't thought any outside threats would be able to get to them. He hadn't realized that the greatest danger was already inside those gates. Hell, inside those brick walls. Had one of his men—one of the O'Hannigan family—set the bomb?

He'd been trying to convince her that he'd had nothing to do with the attempts on her life, years ago or recently. And personally, he hadn't. But that didn't mean he still wasn't responsible...because of who he was.

As if she'd been reading his mind, she softly remarked, "No place, with you, is going to be safe for us."

But he wasn't only the head of a mob organization. He had another life, but, regrettably, that one was probably even more dangerous.

"Where are we?" she asked, pitching her voice to a low whisper—and not just because CJ slept peacefully now in his father's arms, but also because the big brick building was eerily silent.

There had been other vehicles inside the fenced and gated parking lot when they'd arrived. But few lights had glowed in the windows of what looked like an apartment complex. Of course everyone could have been sleeping. But when Brendan had entered a special code to open the doors, the lobby inside looked more commercial than residential.

Was this an office building?

He'd also needed a code to open the elevator doors and a key to turn it on. Fortunately, he'd retrieved his keys from the lock at the mansion...just before the house had exploded.

Her ears had finally stopped ringing. Still, she heard nothing but their footsteps on the terrazzo as they walked down the hallway of the floor on which he'd stopped the elevator. He'd been doing everything with one hand, his arms wrapped tight around their sleeping son.

At the hospital she'd suspected that Brendan had held their son so that she wouldn't try to escape with him. Now he held him almost reverently, as if he was scared that he'd nearly lost him in the explosion.

If he had parked closer to the house...

She shuddered to think what could have happened to her son.

"It'll be warmer inside," Brendan assured her, obviously misinterpreting her shudder as a shiver.

She actually was cold. The building wasn't especially well heated.

"Inside what? Where are we?" she asked, repeating her earlier question. When he'd told her to grab her overnight bag, which she had slung over her shoulder along with her purse, she'd thought he was bringing them to a hotel. But this building was nothing like any hotel at which she'd ever stayed, as Josie Jessup or as JJ Brandt.

"This is my apartment," he said as he stopped outside a tall metal door.

"Apartment? But you had the mansion..." And this building was farther from the city than the house had been, farther from the businesses rumored to be owned or run by the O'Hannigan family. But maybe that was why he'd wanted it—to be able to get away from all the responsibilities he'd inherited.

"I already had this place before I inherited the house from my father," he explained as he shoved the key into the lock.

She wanted to grab her son and run. But she recognized she could just be having a panic attack, like the ones the nightmares brought on when they awakened her in a cold sweat. And those panic attacks, when she ran around checking the house for gas leaks, scared CJ so much that she would rather spare him having to deal with her hysteria tonight.

So she just grabbed Brendan's hand, stilling it before he could turn the key. "We can't stay here!"

Panic rushed up on her, and she dragged in a deep breath to control it and to check the air for that telltale odor. She smelled smoke on them, but it was undoubtedly from the earlier explosion. "Someone could remember you lived here and find us."

"No. It's safe here," he said. "There's no bomb."

"Bu—"

Rejecting her statement before he even heard it, he shook his head. "Nobody knows where I was living before I showed up at my father's funeral."

Some had suspected he hadn't even been alive; they'd thought that instead of running away, he might have been murdered, like they believed his mother was. Some had refused to believe that he was his father's son, despite his having his father's eyes. The same eyes that her son had.

His stepmother had still demanded a DNA test before she had stopped fighting for control of her dead husband's estate. She hadn't stopped slinging the accusations though. She had obviously been the source of so many of the stories about him, such as the one that Brendan had killed his father for vengeance and money. She had even talked to Josie back then to warn her away from a dangerous man.

Given the battle with his stepmother and the constant media attention, Josie could understand that Brendan would need a quiet place to get away from it all.

And it might have occurred to someone else that he would need such a place.

"But they can find out." Somehow, someone had found out she was alive.

"They didn't," he assured her. "It's safe." And despite her nails digging into the back of his hand, he turned the key.

She held her breath, but nothing happened. Then he turned the knob. And still nothing happened, even as the door opened slightly. She expelled a shaky sigh, but she was still tense, still scared.

Perhaps to reassure her even more, he added, "My name's not on the lease."

Just as her name was not on the title of her vehicle or the deed to her house...

Did Brendan O'Hannigan have other identities as well? But why? What was he hiding?

All those years ago she had suspected plenty and she had dug deep, but had found nothing. *She* had never found this place. Back then she would have been elated if he'd brought her here, since he was more likely to keep his secrets in a clandestine location. But when he pushed the door all the way open and stepped back for her to enter, she hesitated.

There was no gas. No bomb. No fire. Nothing to stop her from stepping inside but her own instincts.

"You lost your can of mace," he said. "You can't spray me in the face like you intended."

She gasped in surprise that he'd realized her intentions back at the mansion. "Why didn't you take it from me?"

He shrugged. "By the time I noticed you held it, I was distracted."

He must have smelled the gas, too.

"And then you were saving me instead of hurting me," he reminded her with a smile. "If you were really afraid of me, if you really wanted me gone from your life, you could have just let me blow up."

She glanced down at the child he held so tenderly in his arms. "I—I couldn't do that."

No matter how much she might fear him, she didn't hate him. She didn't want him dead.

"Why?" he asked, his eyes intense as he stared at her over the child in his arms.

"I—I…"

Her purse vibrated, the cell phone inside silently ringing.

"You lost the mace but you didn't lose your phone," he remarked. "You can answer it."

She fumbled inside and pulled out the phone. *That* phone, so it had to be Charlotte. Earlier Josie had wanted desperately to talk to the former marshal. But now she hesitated, as she paused outside his secret place.

"You need to talk to your handler," Brendan advised. "Tell him—"

"Her," she automatically corrected him. But she didn't add that technically she no longer had a handler. When the marshals had failed to find any evidence of his involvement in the attempts on her life, they'd determined they no longer needed to protect her. "Her name is Charlotte Green." Despite neither of them really being associated with the marshals any longer, the woman continued to protect Josie—if only from afar.

"Tell her that you're safe," he said. And as if to give her privacy, he carried their son across the threshold and inside the apartment.

Josie followed him with her gaze but not her body. She hesitated just inside the doorway, but finally she clicked the talk button on the phone. "Charlotte?"

"JJ, I've been so worried about you!" the other woman exclaimed.

That made two of them. But Josie hadn't been worried about just herself. She watched Brendan lay their child on a wide, low sofa. It was a darker shade of gray than the walls and cement floor. But the whole place was monochromatic, which was just different shades of drab to her.

Despite what he'd said, the space didn't look much like an apartment and nothing like a home. As if worried that the boy would roll off the couch and strike the floor, Brendan laid down pillows next to him. He might have just discovered that he was a father, but he had good paternal instincts. He was a natural protector.

And no matter what she'd read or suspected about him, Josie had actually always felt safe with him. Protected. Despite thinking that she should have feared him or at least not trusted him, she'd struggled to come up with a specific reason why. She had no proof that he'd ever tried to hurt her.

Or anyone else.

Maybe all those stories about him had only been stories—told by a bitter woman who'd been disinherited by a heartless and unpitying man.

"JJ?" the female voice emanated from her phone as Charlotte prodded her for a reply.

"I'm okay," she assured the former marshal and current friend.

"And CJ?" Charlotte asked after the boy who'd been named for her.

She had been in the delivery room, holding Josie's

hand, offering her support and encouragement. She hadn't just relocated Josie and left her. Even after she'd left the U.S. Marshals, she had remained her friend.

But the past six months Charlotte hadn't called or emailed, hadn't checked in with Josie at all, almost as if she'd forgotten about her.

"Is CJ okay?" Charlotte asked again, her voice cracking with concern for her godson.

"He had a scare," Josie replied, "but he's safe." While she wasn't entirely sure how safe she really was with him, she had no doubt that Brendan would protect his son.

The other woman cursed. "They found you? That was part of the reason I haven't been calling."

Betrayal struck Josie with all the force of one of the bullets fired at her that evening. "You knew someone was looking for me?"

If Josie had had any idea, she wouldn't have risked bringing CJ to meet his grandfather. Maybe Josie had trusted the wrong person all these years....

"I only just found that out a few weeks ago," Charlotte explained. "Before that I had been unreachable for six months."

"Unreachable?" Her journalistic instincts told her there was more to the story, and Josie wanted to know all of it. "Why were you unreachable?"

"Because I was kidnapped."

She gasped. "Kidnapped?"

"Yes," Charlotte replied, and the phone rattled as if she'd shuddered. "I was kidnapped and held in a place you know about. You mentioned it to Gabby."

"Serenity House?" It was the private psychiatric hospital where Josie's former student had been killed pursuing the story she'd suggested to him. She had known there were suspicious things happening there. She just hadn't imagined how dangerous a place it was. Guilt churned in her stomach; maybe Brendan had had a good reason for being so angry with her. Her stories, even the ones she hadn't personally covered, always caused problems—sometimes even costing lives.

"I'm fine now," Charlotte assured her. "And so is Gabby."

"Was she there, too?" Princess Gabriella St. Pierre was Charlotte's sister and Josie's friend. Josie had gotten to know her over the years through emails and phone calls.

"No, but she was in danger, too," Charlotte replied.

And Josie felt even guiltier for doubting her friend. "No wonder I haven't heard from either of you." They'd been busy, as she had just been, trying to stay alive.

"We think we've found all the threats to our lives," Charlotte said. "But in the process, we found a threat to yours. My former partner—"

Josie shuddered as she remembered the creepy gray-haired guy who had called himself Trigger. Because Josie hadn't felt safe around him, Charlotte had made certain that he wasn't aware of where she had been relocated.

"He was trying to find out where you are."

She hadn't liked or trusted the older marshal, and apparently her instincts had been right. "Why?"

Charlotte paused a moment before replying, "I think someone paid him to learn your whereabouts."

"Who? Did he tell you?"

"No, Whit was forced to kill him to protect Aaron."

Whit and his friend Aaron had once protected Josie. They were the private bodyguards her father had hired after the accident caused by the cut brake lines. But then Whit had discovered the bomb and involved the marshals. He had helped Charlotte stage Josie's death and relocate her. But no one had wanted to put Aaron in the position of lying to her grieving father, so he'd been left thinking he had failed a client. He and Whit had dissolved their security business and their friendship and had gone their separate ways until Charlotte had brought them back together to protect the king of St. Pierre.

"I would have called and warned you immediately," the former marshal said, "but I didn't want to risk my phone being tapped and leading them right to you."

So something must have happened for her to risk it. "Why have you called now?"

"I saw the news about your father," Charlotte said, her voice soft with sympathy. She hadn't understood how close Josie had been to her father, but she'd commiserated with her having to hurt him when she'd faked her death. "I wanted to warn you that it's obviously a ploy to bring you out of hiding."

"Obviously," Josie agreed.

Charlotte gasped. "You went?"

"It was a trap," Josie said, stating the obvious. "But we're fine now." Or so she hoped. "But please check on my dad." The man who had fired at them in the garage was probably the one Brendan had left alive on the sixth floor. He could have gone back to her father's room. "Make sure my dad is okay. Make sure he's safe."

"I already followed up with the hospital," she said. "He's recovering. He'll be fine. And I think he'll stay fine as long as you stay away from him."

Pain clutched Josie's heart. But she couldn't argue

with her friend. She never should have risked going to the hospital.

"You're in extreme danger," Charlotte warned her. "Whoever's after you won't stop now that they know you're alive."

They wouldn't stop until she was dead for real.

"You have no idea who it could be?" Josie asked. She'd never wanted the facts more than she did now.

"It has to be someone with money," Charlotte said, "to pay off a U.S. marshal."

Josie shivered. It wasn't any warmer in Brendan's apartment than it was in the hall. But even if it had been, her blood still would have run cold. "And hire several assassins."

Charlotte gasped. "Several?"

"At least three," she replied. "More if you count whoever set the bomb."

"Bomb!" Charlotte's voice cracked on the exclamation.

"We're fine," Josie reminded her. "But whoever's after me must have deep pockets."

"It's probably O'Hannigan," Charlotte suggested. And she'd no sooner uttered his name than the phone was snapped from Josie's hand.

Brendan had it now, pressed to his ear, as the former U.S. marshal named him as suspect number one. Charlotte hadn't been wrong about anything else. She probably wasn't wrong about this, either.

Chapter Nine

"If you hurt her, I will track you down—"

He chuckled at the marshal's vitriolic threat. And *he* had been accused of getting too personally involved in his job.

Of course, this time he had. But then no one else had been able to take on the assignment. Maybe that was why his father had left him everything. Because Dennis O'Hannigan had known that if anyone ever dared to murder him, Brendan would be the only person capable of bringing his killer to justice.

He couldn't share any of this with Josie though, not with the risk that she would go public with the information. Risk? Hell, certainty. It would be the story of her career. So he stepped inside his den and closed the door behind him, leaving her standing over their sleeping son.

"I'll be easy to find," he assured the marshal. "And I suspect that if anyone gets hurt in my involvement with Josie, it'll be me." Just like last time. And he began to explain to her why he couldn't trust the journalist but why she could trust him.

Of course the marshal was no fool and asked for names and numbers to verify his story. Her thoroughness gave him comfort that she'd been the one protecting Josie all these years. But then she made an admission of her own—that she was no longer on the job.

"What the hell!" he cursed, wishing now that he'd checked her out before he'd told her what so few other people knew. "I thought you had clearance—"

"I do. Through my current security detail, I still have all my clearances and contacts," she assured him. "But as you know, that doesn't mean I couldn't be corrupted like so many others have been."

She was obviously suggesting that he may have been.

"Call those numbers," he urged her.

"I will," she promised. "I will also keep protecting Josie. I can't trust anyone else. That's why I insisted she stay in hiding even after the marshals deemed she wasn't really a witness and withdrew their protection. I had to make certain she stayed safe."

"Why?" he wondered. Then he realized why she'd threatened him, why she cared so much: Josie had become her friend. Hell, the *C* of CJ's name, for Charles, was probably for her.

But her answer surprised him when she replied, "Because of you."

"Because of me?"

"You're part of a powerful family," she reminded him needlessly. "You have unlimited resources of both money and manpower. Josie said several gunmen came after her tonight and someone had set a bomb."

"And those gunmen were shooting at me, too," he said. "And the bomb was set at *my* house."

She sucked in an audible breath of shock.

"I would *never* hurt her," Brendan promised. "I can't

believe she thought that I would." After everything they'd shared...

He hadn't given her a declaration of his feelings, but he had shown her over and over how he felt. Despite his tough assignment, he'd let her distract him. Of course his superiors had authorized it, saying his having a relationship helped establish his cover—that he would have been more suspicious had he remained on his own.

But hell, he'd been on his own most of his life. He was used to that.

"I protected her and CJ tonight," he said. "Hell, I would have died for her—for them." He had wound up having to kill for them instead.

Silence followed his vehement declaration. It lasted so long that he thought he might have lost the connection. Maybe the marshal had hung up on him.

Then she finally spoke again. "I think I know why you wouldn't hurt her, and it has nothing to do with what you've just told me and everything to do with what you *haven't* told me."

Maybe the cell connection was bad, because the woman seemed to make no sense. "What?"

"You love her."

He'd thought so. Once. But then he'd learned the truth about her and why she'd tried so hard to get close to him. "I can't love someone I can't trust."

She laughed now. "I thought that once, too."

"But you fell anyway?"

"No," she said. "My husband did—once Aaron understood my reasons for keeping things from him. He realized that I was only doing my job. Josie will understand when you tell her the truth."

"I can't trust her with the truth," he said.

Charlotte's sigh rattled the phone. "Then you won't be able to make her trust you, either."

"Tell her that she can," Brendan implored her. "She trusts you."

"For a good reason," Charlotte said. "I tell her the truth. And I need to call these people you've given me numbers for and check out your story. Once I do, I'll call Josie back, but I'm not sure she'll take my word without proof. She's been afraid of you for a long time."

Brendan's heart clutched at the thought of the woman he'd once loved living in fear of him, thinking that he would kill her if he found out she was still alive. Maybe he was more like his old man than he'd realized. He clicked off the cell phone and opened the door to his den, half expecting to find Josie listening outside.

But the apartment was eerily silent. Charlotte was right. He couldn't make Josie trust him. And now he didn't have the chance because she'd taken their son and run.

JOSIE WASN'T AS strong as Brendan. She couldn't carry her son, her purse and the backpack with their overnight clothes and toys, and struggle with the special locks and security panels. So she had awakened CJ for an impromptu game of hide-and-seek.

But she hoped Brendan never found them.

CJ was too tired to play though. The poor child had had such a traumatic day that he was physically and emotionally exhausted. He leaned heavily against Josie's legs, nearly knocking her over as she stood near the elevator panel.

She realized that even if she had picked up the code Brendan had punched in, she didn't have the key to work the elevator. He had shoved it back into his pocket.

So she abandoned the elevator and searched for the door to a stairwell. But they were all tall metal doors that looked the same. They could have been apartments. If this place were really an apartment complex…

Its austereness had Josie imagining what Serenity House must have been like. It had her feeling the horror that Charlotte must have felt when she'd been held hostage for six months.

Did Brendan intend to keep her here that long? Longer?

She kept pressing on doors but none of them opened. All were locked to keep her out. Or to keep other people inside?

"Mommy, I wanna go to bed," CJ whined.

"I know, sweetheart." Josie was exhausted, too. She wished she were under the covers of her soft bed and that this whole night had been a horrible nightmare.

But the smoke smell clung to her clothes and hair, proving that it hadn't been a dream. It had happened— every horrible moment of it had been real. She lifted the sleepy child in her arms. For once he didn't protest being carried but laid his head on her shoulder.

"I'm scared, Mommy."

"I know." *Me, too.* But she couldn't make that admission to him. She had to stay strong for them both.

"I wanna go home!"

Me, too. Finally one of the doors opened, and she nearly pitched forward, down the stairs. She'd found the stairwell. Her feet struck each step with an echoing thud as she hurried down. Her arms ached from the weight of the child she carried, and her legs began to tremble in exhaustion.

A crack of metal echoed through the stairwell as a door opened with such force it must have slammed against the wall. Then footsteps, heavier than hers, rang out as someone ran down the steps above her. She quickened her pace. But with CJ in her arms, she couldn't go too fast and risk tumbling down the stairs with him.

Finally she reached the bottom and pushed open the door to the lobby. There was no desk. No security. Nothing but the door with its security lock. She pressed against the outside doors, but they wouldn't open.

Footsteps crossed the lobby behind her. With a sigh of resignation, she turned to face Brendan.

"ARE YOU GOING to stop running from me now?" he asked as she stepped from his den and rejoined him and CJ in the living room. He hated seeing that look on her face, the one he'd seen at the hospital and again in the lobby—that mixture of fear and dread swirling in her smoky-green eyes.

Because of his last name, a lot of people looked at him with fear and he'd learned to not let it bother him. But he didn't want her or their son looking at him that way.

While she'd been on the phone with the former marshal, he had made progress with CJ. Before she'd made her call, she'd given the boy a bath and changed him into his pajamas for bed. So Brendan had told the child a bedside story that his mother used to tell him. The story had lulled the boy to sleep in his arms.

Of course the kid had been totally exhausted, too. But even as tired as he'd been, CJ had kept fighting to keep his eyes open and watchful of Brendan. If a three-year-old couldn't trust him, he probably had no hope of getting a woman, who'd actually witnessed him losing his temper, to trust him.

He eased CJ from his arms onto the couch and then stood up to face the boy's mother. His son's mother. She'd been carrying his baby when she'd disappeared. If only she could have trusted him then…

Obviously still distrustful, Josie narrowed her eyes with suspicion. "What did you tell Charlotte?"

He expelled a quick breath of relief. He hadn't known if he could trust the former U.S. marshal to keep his secrets. Out of professional courtesy she should have. But then, obviously, there wasn't always any communication or respect between the different agencies. And she was no longer with the marshals.

Unable to suppress a slight grin, he innocently asked, "What do you mean?"

She moved her hand, beckoning him inside the den with her so that they wouldn't awaken the child. At this point, Brendan wasn't sure anything—even another explosion—could wake the exhausted boy. But he stepped away from the couch and joined her.

She closed the door behind her and leaned against it with her hands wrapped around the handle, as if she might need to make a quick getaway. After her last attempt, she should have realized she wouldn't easily escape this complex.

He should have brought her and his son here immediately. But since she'd already been in witness protection, he'd worried that she might recognize a "safe" house and question, as she questioned everything, why he had access to one.

"You know what I mean," she said, her voice sharp

with impatience. "What did you say to make Charlotte Green trust you?"

The truth. But that wasn't something with which he could trust Stanley Jessup's daughter. He shrugged as if he wasn't sure. "What I told her doesn't really matter. I think it would take a lot more to make you trust me than her."

"True." She nodded in agreement. "Because I know you better than Charlotte does."

Images flashed through his mind, of how she knew him. She knew how to kiss him and touch him to make him lose control. She knew how to make love with him so that he forgot all his responsibilities and worries, so that he thought only of her. And even during all the years she was gone, he'd thought of her. He'd mourned her.

He stepped closer so that she pressed her back against the door. He only had to lean in a few more inches to close the distance between them, to press his body against hers, to show her that she still got to him, that he still wanted her.

His voice was husky with desire when he challenged, "Do you?"

Her pupils darkened as she stared up at him and her voice was husky as she replied, "You know I do."

Were those images of their entwined naked bodies running through her mind, too? Was she remembering how it felt when he was inside her, as close as two people could get?

She cleared her throat and emphatically added, "I know you."

"No." He shook his head. "If you did, you would have known I wasn't the one who tried to kill you three years ago."

"But you were so angry with me.…"

"I was," he agreed. "You were lying to me and tricking me."

"But I didn't steal from you." She defended herself from what he'd told their son earlier.

She had stolen from him; she just didn't know it. She'd stolen his heart.

But he just shrugged. "My trust…"

"I guess that went both ways," she said.

"You never trusted me," he pointed out. "Or you would have known you wouldn't find the story you were after, that I'm not the man my father was."

She leaned wearily against the door, as if she were much older than she was. "I never found the story," she agreed. "And I gave up so much for it."

She had given up the only life she'd known. Her home. Her family. Brendan could relate to that loss.

Then a small smile curved her lips and she added, "But I got the most important thing in my life."

"Our son?"

She nodded. "That's why I have to be careful who I trust. It's why I have to leave here."

"You're safe here," he assured her. Only people who knew what he really was knew about this place. Until tonight, when he'd taken her here.

She shook her head. "Not here. CJ and I need to go home. We've been safe there. I know I can keep him safe."

He appreciated that she was a protective mother. "You don't have to do that alone anymore."

"I haven't," she said. "I had Charlotte. She was even in the delivery room with me."

That was why Josie had named their son after the U.S. marshal.

"She's too far away to help you now," he pointed out. "That's why she told you to—" he stepped closer and touched her face, tipping her chin up so she would meet his gaze "—let me."

She stared up at him, her eyes wide as if she were searching. For what?

Goodness? Honor?

He wasn't certain she would find them no matter how hard she looked. In his quest for justice for his father, he had had to bury deep any signs of human decency—at least when he was handling business. When he'd been with her, he'd let down his guard. He'd been himself even though he hadn't told her who he was.

"What would I have to say to you," he asked, "to make you trust me?"

"Whatever you told Charlotte," she said. "Tell me what you told her."

He shook his head. "I can't trust you with that information."

She jerked her chin from his hand as if unable to bear his touch any longer. "But you expect me to trust *you*—not with just my life, but CJ's, too."

She had a point. But he'd worked so long, given up so much.

If only she hadn't lied to him…

He flinched over her disdainful tone. "Why would I be more untrustworthy than anyone else?"

"Like you don't know why," she said.

"Because of who I am?"

"Because of *what* you are."

Charlotte had definitely not told her anything that he had shared with the former U.S. marshal.

"What am I?"

"I never got my story about you," she said, "because

you never answered my questions. But I need you to answer at least one if you expect me to stay here."

He nodded in agreement. "I'll answer one," he replied. "But how do you know I'll tell you the truth?"

"Swear on your mother's grave."

He wouldn't need to tell her the truth then, because his mother wasn't dead. Like everyone else, he had believed she'd been murdered when he was just a kid. But she was actually the first person he'd known who'd entered witness protection. The marshals hadn't let her take him along, forcing her to leave a child behind with a man many had considered a psychopath as well as her killer.

If Brendan hadn't run away when he was fifteen, he might have never learned the truth about either of his parents.

"Do you swear?" she prodded him. "Will you answer me honestly?"

"Yes," he agreed, and hoped like hell he wouldn't have to lie to her. But no matter what he'd promised her, he couldn't tell her what he really was. "What do you want to know?"

"Before tonight, before those men on the roof—" she shuddered as though remembering the blood and the gunshots "—have you killed anyone else?"

He had promised her the truth, so he answered truthfully. "Yes."

Chapter Ten

He was a killer. Maybe she should have believed everything she had heard and read about him—even the unsubstantiated stories.

"But just like tonight, it was in self-defense," he explained, his deep voice vibrating with earnestness and regret, as though killing hadn't been easy for him. "I have only killed when there's been no other option, when it's been that person's life or mine, or the life of an innocent person." He flinched as if reliving some of those moments. "Like you or our son."

"You've been in these life-and-death situations before tonight," she said.

He nodded.

"How many times?" she asked. "Twice? Three times?"

"I agreed to answer only one question," he reminded her.

She swallowed hard, choking on the panic she felt just thinking of all the times he'd been in danger, all the times he could have died. "And you were trying to say I was responsible for what happened tonight. And for the attempts on my life years ago. You're the one leading the dangerous life."

He stepped back from her and sighed. "You're right."

She appealed to him. "So you need to let us leave, to let me go home."

"I can't do that."

"How can you expect to keep me and CJ safe when you're always fighting for your own life?" she asked.

He stripped off his suit jacket. Despite the crazy night they'd had, it was barely wrinkled, but he carelessly dropped it on the floor. And in doing so, he revealed the holsters strapped across his broad shoulders, a gun under each heavily muscled arm. She'd already known about the concealed weapons; she'd already seen all of his guns. Then he reached up and pulled one of those guns from its holster and pointed it toward her.

She gasped and stepped back, but she was already against the door and had no place else to go. Unless she opened the door, but then her son might see that the man he didn't even realize yet was his father was holding a gun on his mother.

"What—what are you doing?" she stammered. "I—I thought you wanted me to trust you."

"That's why I'm giving you this gun," he said. The handle, not the barrel, was pointed toward her. "Take it."

She shook her head. "No."

"Don't you know how to shoot one?"

"Charlotte taught me." The marshal had taken her to the shooting range over and over again until Josie had gotten good at it. "She tried to give me one, too. But I didn't want it."

"You don't like guns?"

Until tonight, when they'd been shooting at her, Josie hadn't had any particular aversion to firearms. "I don't want one in the same house with CJ."

"You can lock it up," Brendan said, "to make sure he doesn't get to it."

"So if I take this gun, you'll let us leave?" she asked, reaching for it. The metal was cold to the touch and heavy across her palms. She identified the safety, grateful it was engaged.

He shook his head. "Until we find out who's trying to kill you, I can't let you or our son out of my sight."

"Then why give me this?"

"So you'll trust me," he said. "If I wanted to hurt you, I wouldn't give you a gun to protect yourself."

She expelled a ragged sigh, letting all her doubts and fears of Brendan go with the breath from her lungs. A bad man wouldn't have given her the means to defend herself from him. Had she been wrong about him all these years?

Had she kept him from his son for no reason?

Guilt descended on her, bowing her shoulders with the heavy burden of it she already carried. For her student, and for that other young man's death she'd inadvertently caused. She hadn't needed Brendan to remind her that there were other people with reason to want to hurt her, as she'd hurt them. She hadn't meant to.

She'd only been after the truth. But sometimes the truth caused more pain than letting secrets remain secret. If only she'd understood that sooner…

"Are you okay?" he asked, his deep voice full of concern.

How could he care about her—after everything she'd thought of him, everything she'd taken from him? He had been right that she'd stolen from him. She had taken away the first three years of his son's life.

Her hands trembled so much that she quickly slid the

gun into her purse so that she wouldn't drop it. "I—I'm fine," she said. "I'm just overwhelmed."

"You're exhausted," he said.

And he was touching her again, his hands on her shoulders. He led her toward the couch. Like the one in the living room, it was wide and low, and as she sank onto the edge of it, it felt nearly as comfortable as a mattress.

Her purse dropped to the floor next to the couch, but she let it go. She didn't need the gun. She didn't need to protect herself from Brendan, at least not physically. But emotionally she was at risk of falling for him all over again.

"You can lie down here," he said. "And I'll keep an eye on CJ."

"He's out cold," she said. Her son wouldn't awaken again before morning. But regrettably that was only a few hours off.

Brendan shook his head. "I can't sleep anyway."

"I can't sleep, either." She reached up and grabbed his hand, tugging him down beside her.

He turned toward her, his eyes intense as he stared at her. The pupils dilated, and his chest—his massively muscled chest—heaved as he drew in an unsteady breath. "Josie…"

"You gave me a gun," she murmured, unbelievably moved by his gesture.

"Most women would prefer flowers or jewelry."

The woman she'd once been would have, but that woman had died nearly four years ago. The woman she was now preferred the gun, preferred that he'd given her the means to protect herself…even from him.

"I'm not most women," she said.

"No," he agreed. "Most women I would have been able to put from my mind. But I never stopped thinking about you—" he reached for her now, touching her chin and then sliding his fingers up her cheek "—never stopped wanting you."

Then his mouth was on hers as he kissed her deeply, his tongue sliding between her lips. She moaned as passion consumed her, heating her skin and her blood.

Her fingers trembled, and she fumbled with the buttons on his shirt. She needed him. After tonight she needed to feel the way he had always made her feel— *alive*.

He caught her fingers as if to stop her. Josie opened her eyes and gasped in protest. But then he replaced her hands with his. He stripped off his holsters and then his shirt, baring his chest for her greedy gaze.

He was beautiful, the kind of masculine perfection that defied reality. That weakened a woman's knees and her resolve. Josie leaned forward and kissed his chest, skimming her lips across the muscles.

Soft hair tickled her skin.

His fingers clenched in her hair, and he gently pulled her back. Then his hands were on her, pulling her sweater over her head and stripping off her bra.

"You're beautiful," he said, his voice gruff.

She wasn't the woman she'd once been, emotionally or physically. She'd worried that he wouldn't look at her as he once had—his face flushed with desire, his nostrils flaring as he breathed hard and fast. But he was looking at her that way now.

"You're even more beautiful," he murmured, "than you once were."

She didn't know whether to be offended, so she

laughed. "Then the marshals didn't get their money's worth from the plastic surgeon."

"It's not an external thing," he said. "You have a beauty that comes from within now."

"It's happiness," she admitted.

"Despite all you had to give up?" His hands skimmed along her jaw again. "Even your face?"

"I have my son," she said, "our son…"

"Our son," he said.

"I'm sorry I didn't tell you I was pregnant," she said, "that I didn't tell you when he was born."

"You didn't trust me," he said. "You thought I wanted to kill you."

"I was wrong." She knew that now. She didn't know everything. He was keeping other things from her—things that he'd shared with Charlotte but wouldn't tell her. But maybe it was better that she didn't know. Maybe the secrets kept her safer than the gun.

He kissed her again, as he had before. Deeply. Passionately. His chest rubbed against her breasts, drawing her nipples to tight points.

She moaned again and skimmed her hands over his back, pressing him closer to her. As she ran her palms down his spine, she hit something hard near his waistband. Something cold and hard.

Another gun.

How many did he have on him?

He stood up and took off that weapon, as well as another on his ankle. Then his belt and pants came off next.

And Josie gasped as desire rushed over her. She had never wanted anyone the way she'd wanted Brendan. Because she'd known she never would, she hadn't gotten involved with anyone else the past four years. She'd focused on being a mother and a teacher and had tried to forget she was a woman.

She remembered now. Her hands trembling, she unclasped her jeans and skimmed them off along with her simple cotton panties. Brendan reached between them and stroked his fingers over her red curls.

Her breath caught. And she clutched his shoulders as her legs trembled.

"You haven't changed completely," he murmured.

He continued to stroke her until she came, holding tight to him so that she didn't crumple to the floor. But then he laid her down on the couch. And he made love to her with his mouth, too, his fingers stroking over her breasts, teasing her nipples until she completely shattered, overcome with ecstasy. But there was more.

She pulled him up her body, stroking her hands and mouth over all his hard, rippling muscles…until his control snapped. And he thrust inside her, filling the emptiness with which she'd lived the past four years.

Their mouths made love like their bodies, tongues tangling, lips skimming, as he thrust deep and deeper. She arched to take all of him. A pressure wound tightly inside her, stretching her, making her ache. She gasped for breath as her heart pounded and her pulse raced.

Then Brendan reached between them; his fingers stroked through those curls and his thumb pressed against that special nub. And she came. So she wouldn't scream, she kissed him more deeply as pleasure pulsed through her.

He groaned deeply into her mouth as his body tensed and he joined her in ecstasy. Pleasure shook his body, just as hers still trembled with aftershocks. But even once their bodies relaxed, he didn't let her go. He wrapped his arms tightly around her, holding her close to his madly pounding heart.

And she felt safe. Protected. For the first time in nearly four years.

FOR THE FIRST time in nearly four years, Brendan didn't feel so alone. Josie had had their son; he had had no one. No one he dared get close to. No one he dared to trust.

Part of that had been her fault. After her subterfuge, he'd been careful to let no other woman get to him. But he suspected that even if he hadn't been careful, no other woman could have gotten to him.

Only Josie…

Maybe Charlotte Green was right. Maybe he did love Josie. And maybe he should trust her. He hadn't noticed any articles she'd written showing up in her father's papers. Maybe she'd stepped away from the media world. Not that her articles had been sensationalized. They had been brutally honest, stripping the subject bare. That was why he would have recognized anything she'd written—her style was distinctive.

But maybe becoming a mother had changed her priorities. Maybe she cared more about keeping CJ hidden than exposing others.

He stroked his fingers over her shoulder and down her bare back. "Your skin is so soft." He'd thought it was because of fancy spa treatments she would have had as American princess Josie Jessup. But with the new lifestyle the marshals would have set up for her, she wouldn't have been able to go to expensive spas.

She would have had to live modestly and quietly, or else she would have been found before now. Because someone was looking for her.

Why?

To get to him?

She was his only weakness. Hurting her would draw him out, and maybe make him careless enough for someone to get the jump on him.

Had she had to give up everything—her home, family and career—because of him? Then she deserved to know the truth.

"Josie…"

"Hmm…" she murmured sleepily.

He looked down at her face and found her eyes closed, her lashes lying on the dark circles beneath. And her body was limp in his arms, relaxed. He couldn't wake her. After everything she'd been through that night, she needed to rest and recuperate. Because their ordeal wasn't over yet. It wouldn't be over until he discovered who was trying to kill her.

But they were safe now, here, wrapped in each other's arms, so he closed his eyes.

He didn't know how long he'd been asleep when the alarm sounded. No, the piercing whistle was not from a clock but from the security panel in the den.

"What!" Josie exclaimed as she jerked awake in his arms. "What is that?"

"Security has been breached," he said, already reaching for his clothes and his weapons.

There were other apartments inside the building, other witnesses or suspects or agents the intruder could have been after. But Brendan knew the alarm was for them—the danger coming for them.…

He had just one question for her. "How well do you know how to shoot?"

Chapter Eleven

While she'd held the gun when he'd handed it to her, the weight of it was still unfamiliar in her hands. Before tonight she hadn't held one in years, let alone fired one. And when she had fired one, it had only been at targets—not people.

Could she pull the trigger on a person?

"Mommy, the 'larm clock is too loud," CJ protested with his tiny hands tightly pressed against his ears.

Brendan scooped him up and headed toward the apartment door. "Grab your stuff," he told her over his shoulder. He carried the boy with one arm while he clutched a gun in his other hand.

"Sh-shouldn't we stay here?" she asked. "And just lock the door?"

His turquoise eyes intense, he shook his head. "We don't know if the breach was someone getting inside or *putting* something inside."

A bomb.

Josie gasped and hurried toward the door. But she slammed into Brendan's back as he abruptly stopped.

"We have to be very quiet," he warned them.

"CJ, you have to play statue," she told their son. "No matter what happens, you have to be quiet."

"Like on the roof?"

Not like that. She wouldn't dare leave her little boy alone in the dark again. "Well…"

"We're all staying together," Brendan said, "and we're staying quiet."

She released a shaky sigh.

"Mommy, shh," the little boy warned her.

A corner of Brendan's mouth lifted in a slight grin. Then he slowly opened the door. He nodded at her before stepping into the hall. It was clear. He wouldn't have brought their son into the line of fire.

But they needed to get out of the building. Fast.

She breathed deep, checking for the telltale odor of gas. But she smelled nothing but Brendan; the scent of his skin clung to hers. While they'd been making love, someone had gotten inside the building.

What if that person had gotten inside the apartment? He or they could have grabbed CJ before his parents had had a chance to reach him.

Her heart ached with a twinge of guilt more powerful than any she'd felt before. And she'd felt plenty guilty over the years.

She followed after Brendan, watching as he juggled the boy and his gun. "If we're taking the elevator…"

He would need to give her the code to punch into the security panel. But he shook his head and pushed open the door to the stairwell.

Of course they wouldn't want to be in the elevator. If the building exploded, they would be trapped. But wouldn't they be trapped inside the stairwell, too? If the gunmen were heading up, they would meet them on the way down—and CJ would be caught in the crossfire.

Brendan didn't hesitate though. He hurried down the first flight and then the second.

"Brendan…"

Over his father's shoulder, their little boy pressed a finger to his lips, warning her again to be quiet.

They had stopped, but their footsteps echoed. Then she realized it wasn't their footsteps that were echoing. It was someone else's—on their way up, as she'd feared. But Brendan continued to go down.

"No," she whispered frantically. "They're coming!"

He stopped on the next landing and pushed open the door to the hall. "Run," he told her.

"To the elevator?" They could take it now. The men wouldn't have come inside if they'd set a bomb.

"No," he said. "Door at the end of the hall. Go through it." He pushed her ahead of him and turned back as the door to the stairwell opened. But he kept his back toward that door, his body between their son and whoever might exit the stairwell. Before anyone emerged, he fired and kept firing as he ran behind Josie.

She pushed through that door he'd pointed at and burst onto a landing with such force that she nearly careened over the railing of the fire escape. Brendan, CJ clutched tight against his chest, exited behind her.

He momentarily holstered his gun, even though the men had to be right behind him, and he grabbed up a pipe that lay on the landing and slid it through the handle, jamming the door shut.

How had he known the pipe was there? Had he planned such an escape before?

The door rattled as another body struck it.

"Go," he told her. "Run!"

She nearly stumbled as she hurried down the dimly illuminated metal steps. But gunfire rang out again—shots fired against that jammed door.

Brendan, still holding their son, who was softly sobbing, rushed down the stairs behind her. The shots, the urgency, the danger had her trembling so uncontrollably that she slipped, her feet flying from beneath her.

She would have fallen, would have hit each metal step on the long way to the ground. But a strong hand caught her arm, holding her up while she regained her footing.

When they neared the bottom of the fire escape, the gun was back in his hand, the light from the parking lot lamps glinting off the metal.

She hadn't lost the gun she'd carried. She hadn't used it, either, and wasn't even sure that she could. But then she heard a car door open and a gun cock.

And she knew that someone had a clear shot at them. So she slid off the safety and turned with the gun braced in both hands. But before she could squeeze the trigger, a shot rang out and she heard a windshield shatter.

"Come on," Brendan urged her. "Your car's over here. Hurry."

"But—"

There was a shooter in the lot. Or had Brendan already shot him? The gun was in his free hand while his other hand clasped their son to his chest.

"Do you have the keys?" he asked.

She pulled them out of her purse and clicked the key fob. Lights flashed on the SUV, guiding them to it and also revealing it to the gunmen as they erupted from the lobby of the building.

This time she squeezed the trigger, shooting at the men pointing guns at her son and the man she loved. The weapon kicked back, straining her wrist.

"Get in!" Brendan yelled as he put their boy into the backseat. "Buckle him up!"

She dropped the gun into her bag and jumped into the passenger's seat. As she leaned over the console and buckled up their son, Brendan was already careening out of the lot.

"Stay down!" he yelled at her, just as more shots rang out. Bullets pinged and tires squealed.

And their son continued to play statue, staying silent in the backseat. "You're so brave," she praised him, reaching back to touch his face.

His chin quivered and she felt moisture on her fingers—probably his tears. But he had his eyes squeezed tightly shut, trying not to cry. She pulled back her hand and studied what was smeared across her fingers. It wasn't tears. It was something red and sticky. Blood.

"Brendan! He's hurt!" she exclaimed, fear and dread clutching her heart in a tight vise. "Get to the hospital! Call the police!"

"No," HE CORRECTED her as blood trickled down his temple. "CJ wasn't hit." He'd made damn certain of that.

"Th-there's blood on his face," she said, her voice shaking with fear and anger.

Brendan tipped the rearview mirror and studied their son in the backseat. The little boy scrubbed at his face and held up a hand sticky with blood. "It's not mine, Mommy. It came off…" His son didn't know what to call him, didn't know who he was to him.

"Your daddy," Brendan answered the boy. "I'm your daddy."

Josie gasped, probably at his audacity for telling their child who he was. But then she was reaching across the console and touching his head. "Where are you hit?"

"Daddy?" CJ asked.

Brendan's head pounded. He wanted to pull off the road, wanted to explain to his son who he was, wanted to let Josie touch him. But he had to tip the mirror back up and check the road behind them. Had anyone followed them?

He'd thought he'd been vigilant on his way from the estate to the complex, that he hadn't been followed. Had he missed a tail?

With blood trickling into his eyes, he was more likely to miss one now, so he asked Josie, "Do you see anything?"

Her fingers stroked through his hair. "No. Where were you hit?"

He shook his head, and the pain radiated, making him wince. "I wasn't hit," he replied, lifting his fingers to his left temple. "I was grazed. It's just a scratch." A scratch that stung like a son of a bitch, but he ignored the pain and focused on the road. "Is there anyone behind us?"

"What?" She must have realized what he was referring to, because she turned around and peered out the rear window. "I don't see any other lights."

The roads were deserted this early in the morning. He passed only a garbage truck going the other direction. No one was behind him. No one had been behind him earlier, either. He blinked back the trickle of blood and remarked, "I was not followed to the complex."

"So how did they find us?" she asked.

"Daddy?" CJ repeated from the backseat, interrupting them. "You're my daddy?"

Josie sucked in an audible breath as if just noticing

that Brendan had told their son who he was. He waited to see if she would deny it now, if she would call him a liar for claiming his child. If she did, he would call her on the lie. After his close call with that bullet, he wanted his son to know who he was…before it was too late. Before he never got the chance to tell him.

Josie turned toward the backseat and offered their son a shaky smile. "Yes, sweetheart, he's your daddy."

"I—I thought he was a bad man."

Josie shook her head. "No, sweetheart, he's a good man. A hero. He keeps saving us from the bad men."

Was she saying that for the boy's sake? To make CJ feel better? Safer? Or did she believe it? Had she finally really come to trust Brendan, even though he hadn't told her the truth?

"My daddy…" the little boy murmured, as if he were falling back to sleep. Given that his slumber kept getting violently interrupted, it was no wonder that the little boy was still tired.

"Well, we know who I am," Brendan said. A hero? Did she really see him that way? "What about who's after us?"

She kept staring into the backseat as if watching her son to make sure that the blood really wasn't his. Or that the news of his parentage hadn't affected him.

"Whoever it is," he said, "appears to want us both dead."

"They're gone," she murmured. Apparently she'd been watching the back window instead. "We're safe now."

"We should have been safe where we were," he replied. It was a damn *safe* house.

"We need to go home," she murmured, sounding as dazed as their son. But she wasn't just tired; she was probably in shock. She'd fired her gun at people. If that had been the first time, she was probably having an emotional reaction. She was trembling and probably not just because the car had yet to warm up. "We need to go home," she repeated.

She wasn't talking about his home. Neither the mansion where he'd grown up nor the apartment where he'd spent much of his adult life was safe. But she couldn't be talking about her place, either.

Maybe her father's? But if the news reports were correct, he'd been attacked in the parking garage of his condominium complex.

"We can't," he said. "It's not safe at your dad's, either."

"We have to go home," she said, her voice rising slightly now, as if with hysteria. "To what CJ and I call home, where we've been living."

"Don't you get it?" he asked. "The only one who could have tracked down where we were was your *friend.*"

She leaned forward and peered into his face as if worried that the bullet had impaired his thinking. "Friend?"

"The former marshal," he said. "She must have traced the call to where we were staying. She sent those people." It couldn't have been anyone else. Damn! Why had he trusted the woman?

Josie sucked in an audible breath of shock. "Charlotte? You think Charlotte is behind the attempts on my life?"

"No." He knew she considered the woman a friend, at one point maybe her only friend. And she had to be devastated. But she also had to know the truth. "But she must have sold out to whoever wants you dead."

Josie chuckled. Maybe she'd given over completely to hysteria and shock. "You think Charlotte Green sold out?"

He nodded, and his head pounded again. "It had to be her. You can't trust her."

"She told me to trust you," she reminded him. "So now you're saying that I shouldn't?"

"No, no," he said. "You should trust me but not her. Remember what you told our son—I'm not a bad man. I've saved you."

Something jammed into his ribs, and he glanced down. She held the gun he'd given her, not just on him but nearly in him as she pushed the barrel into his side. After the night she'd had, he could understand her losing it. But was she irrational enough to pull the trigger?

Had she slid off the safety? If he hit a bump in the road, she might squeeze the trigger. She might shoot him and then he might crash the SUV and take them all out.

He hadn't realized that he might need to protect Josie from herself.

HE WAS LOOKING at her nervously, as if he worried that she'd lost her mind. Maybe she had.

Could she do it? Could she pull the trigger? If she had to... If killing Brendan was necessary to save her life or CJ's.

But she believed what she'd told their son. He was a hero—at least he had been their hero—time and time again the past night. Moreover, she believed in him.

She had the safety on the gun, in case there were any bullets left in it. She hoped like hell there were none. But with Brendan looking as nervous as he was, he obviously thought there could be.

And he thought she could fire the gun.

Good. That was the only way she was going to co-erce him to take her where she wanted to go. Where she needed to go. Home.

"We're doing things my way now," she said. Since the shoot-out at the hospital, he had brought her from one place to another and neither had been safe.

"You're not going to pull the trigger," he said. "You're not a killer."

She flinched, hoping that was true. She'd fired the gun back at the complex. Had she hit anyone?

She shot back at him with a smart remark. "Guess that makes one of us."

"Then why pull the gun on me if you don't intend to use it?" he asked, his body pressed slightly against the barrel of her gun as if he were beginning to relax. Had he realized that she hadn't gone crazy? That she was just determined?

"I don't want to use it," she admitted, "but I will if you don't take me where I want to go."

"It's too dangerous," he protested. "Since Charlotte gave up our safe house, she sure as hell gave up the place where she relocated you."

"Why?" she asked.

"I told you—for money."

She laughed again. "Do you have any idea who Charlotte Green is?"

He glanced at her with that look again, as if he thought she belonged in a place like Serenity House. "A former U.S. marshal."

"Her father is king of a wealthy island country near Greece," she shared. The last thing Charlotte needed was money. "She's a princess."

"What?" He definitely thought she was crazy now.

"She's Princess Gabriella St. Pierre's sister," she explained. "They're royal heiresses." Of course Charlotte had spent most of her life unaware that she was royalty. Only upon her mother's death had she learned the woman had been the king's mistress and herself his illegitimate heir.

"So are you."

She snorted over the miniscule amount of royal blood running in her veins. Her mother had been a descendent of European royalty, but she'd given up her title to marry Josie's father. "Not anymore," she reminded him. "I gave up that life."

And she shouldn't have risked coming back to it, not even to see her father, because her arrival had only put him in more danger. God, she hoped he was safe. She had asked Charlotte to check on him, to protect him. What if Brendan was actually right about her?

No, that wasn't possible. Charlotte would never betray her.

"I have a *new* home," she said. "And we're going there. It might be the only safe place we have left to go."

"Or it could be a trap," he said. "They could be waiting for us there."

"Charlotte wouldn't have given us up," she said. "She's CJ's godmother. My friend. She wouldn't have given us up."

She barked out directions, and he followed them. She suspected it wasn't because of the gun she pressed into his side but because he had no place else to take her. He'd tried the O'Hannigan mansion and what had probably been some type of safe house. Why had no other tenants come out into the halls when the alarm had sounded? Why had it only been them and the gunmen?

"What if you're wrong about her?" he asked. "What if she's not really who you think she is?"

Then Charlotte wouldn't be the only one she'd mis-judged. Brendan O'Hannigan wasn't who she'd thought he was, either. She had been wrong about him for so long. What if she was wrong about Charlotte, too? What if the marshal had been compromised?

She wouldn't have sold out Josie for money, but she might have sold her out if there was a threat against someone she loved, such as her sister. Or Aaron…

The closer they got to her home, the more scared Josie became that Brendan might be right. They could be walking right into the killer's trap.

Chapter Twelve

Brendan could have taken the gun away from her at any time. He could have snapped it out of her hand more easily than he had taken the weapon off the faux orderly who'd grabbed him on the sixth floor. But he hadn't wanted to hurt her. She had already been hurt enough. And if he was right, she was about to be hurt a hell of a lot more.

He intimately knew how painful it was to be betrayed by someone you loved. As a friend, as a lifeline to her old life, she had loved Charlotte Green. And he'd been fool enough to trust the woman with the truth about himself.

But he'd wanted her to convince Josie to trust him. Now Josie held a gun on him, forcing him to bring her back to a trap. Should he trust her?

Was she part of it? Was this all a ploy to take him down? If not for the boy, he might have suspected her involvement in a murder plot against him. But she loved her son. She wouldn't knowingly endanger him.

As he drove north, light from the rising sun streamed through her window, washing her face devoid of all color. Her eyes were stark, wide with fear, in her pale face.

"Are you sure you want to risk it?" he asked.

"You're trying to make me doubt myself," she said. "Trying to make me doubt Charlotte."

"Yes," he admitted.

She looked at him, her eyes filling with sadness and pity. "You don't trust anyone, do you?"

"I shouldn't have," he said. "But I trusted you."

She pulled the gun slightly away from his side. "You gave me this gun."

"The one you're holding on me."

"I wouldn't really shoot you," she assured him, and with a sigh, she dropped the gun back into her purse.

"I know."

"Then why did you come here?" She sat up straighter as they passed a sign announcing the town limits of Sand Haven, Michigan. Another sign stood beyond that, a billboard prompting someone named Michael to rest in peace.

Josie flinched as she read the sign.

"Do you know Michael?" he asked.

She jerked her chin in a sharp nod. "I knew him."

"I'm sorry." Had her recent loss explained why she'd been so desperate to see her father that she'd risked her safety and CJ's?

She hadn't been in contact with her father, as he'd initially expected. The man, who'd looked so sad and old at her funeral, had believed she was dead just as Brendan had.

"You hadn't seen your dad until—" he glanced at the sun rising high in the sky "—last night?"

"I didn't see him last night, either," she said.

"But you were on the right floor," he said, remembering the lie she'd told him.

She bit her lip and blinked hard, as if fighting tears,

before replying, "The assault brought on a heart attack. I didn't want his seeing me to bring on another one."

"So he has no idea that you're really alive?"

She shook her head. "I thought it would be better if he didn't know. I thought he'd be safer."

"You and your father were close," he said. "It must have been hard to leave him."

"Harder to deceive him," she said.

But she'd had no problem deceiving him when she'd been trying to get her story. But then she hadn't loved him.

He drew in a deep breath and focused on the road. She'd given him directions right to her door. Giving her the gun had made her trust him. But she had placed her trust in someone she shouldn't have.

"Let me go in first," he suggested as he drove past the small white bungalow where she lived now. "Let me make sure that it's not a trap."

She shuddered as if she remembered the bomb set at his house. There had been very little left of the brick Tudor; it wouldn't take a very big bomb to totally decimate her modest little home.

He turned the corner and pulled the SUV over to the curb on the next street. After shifting into Park, he reached for the door handle, but she clutched his arm.

Her voice cracking, she said, "I don't want you to go alone."

"You can't go with me," he said. "You have to protect our son."

"If you can't?" She shook her head. "It's not a trap. It can't be a trap." She had been on her own so long that she was desperately hanging on to her trust for the one person who'd been there for her.

He forced a reassuring smile for her sake. "Then I'll be right back."

She stared at him, her eyes wide with uncertainty. She wanted to believe him as much as she wanted to believe that Charlotte hadn't betrayed her.

"I'll be back." He leaned across the console and clasped her face in his hands, tipping her mouth up for his kiss. He lingered over her lips, caressing them slowly and thoroughly. "Wait here for me."

She opened her mouth again, but she made no protest. He opened the driver's door and then opened the backseat door. She turned and looked over the console as he leaned in and pressed a kiss against his son's mussed red curls. The boy never stirred from his slumber.

"Thank you," he said. "Thank you for telling him that I'm his father."

"You told him."

"But you didn't contradict me," he said. "He would have believed what you told him over whatever I told him." Because he loved and trusted his mother. Brendan was a stranger to him. And if he was right about the trap, he may forever remain a stranger to him.

The little boy might grow up never knowing his father.

BRENDAN HAD BEEN gone too long. Longer than he needed to check out the house and make sure it was as safe as she was hoping it was.

But what if it wasn't?

The keys dangled from the ignition. He hadn't taken them this time, because he wasn't sure he'd be coming back. Josie's heart rate quickened, pounding faster with each second that passed.

She needed to go to her house. Needed to check on him.

Or perhaps she should call Charlotte for backup. But he wouldn't need backup unless Charlotte had betrayed them. Panic and dread clutched her heart. Not Charlotte. Not her friend, her son's godmother.

Charlotte couldn't have revealed Josie's new location, not even to protect someone else. But maybe someone had found out anyway. Josie needed to learn the truth.

She wriggled out of the passenger's seat, over the console and behind the steering wheel. Then she turned the keys in the ignition.

CJ murmured as the engine started. He was waking up. She couldn't leave him in the car and she couldn't bring him with her—in case Brendan was right about her house being a trap now.

So she brought her son where she brought him every morning, where she would have brought him that morning if she hadn't taken a leave from work. She drove him to day care. It was only a few blocks from her house, at the home of a retired elementary schoolteacher.

Mrs. Mallory watched CJ and two other preschool children. The sixty-something woman opened the door as Josie carried him up the walk. And the smile on her face became tight with concern the closer Josie came.

"Are you all right?" the older woman anxiously asked.

How awful did she look?

A glance in the mirror by the door revealed dark circles beneath her eyes, and her hair was tangled and mussed, looking as though she'd not pulled a comb through it in days. She probably hadn't.

"I'm fine," Josie assured her. "I'm just in a hurry."

Mrs. Mallory reached out for the sleepy child. "I wasn't even expecting you. I thought you were taking some time off." As she cradled the boy in one arm, she squeezed Josie's shoulder with her other hand. "You really should. Let this whole tragic situation with Michael die down."

"So people are blaming me?"

Mrs. Mallory bit her lip and nodded. "It's not your fault, though, honey. That boy wanted to be a reporter since he wasn't much older than CJ here."

"But I suggested the story...."

"But you didn't pull the trigger," the older woman pointed out. "People are blaming the wrong person and they'll realize that soon enough. Just give them some time. Or take some for yourself."

She had no time to lose—not if Brendan had walked into a trap. "Even though you weren't planning on it, would you mind watching him for a little while?"

"'Course not," the older woman assured her, and she cuddled him close in her arms. She was wearing one of the velour tracksuits that CJ loved snuggling into. "I was just starting to miss him."

CJ lifted his head from Mrs. Mallory's shoulder as if just realizing where he was. "Daddy? Where's my daddy?"

Mrs. Mallory's eyes widened with shock. The boy had never mentioned him before. Of course, before last night he hadn't even known he had a father. Or a grandfather.

"You have to stay here with Mrs. M," Josie told him, leaning forward to press a kiss against his freckled cheek, "and be a good boy, okay?"

His bottom lip began to quiver and his eyes grew

damp with tears he fought back with quick blinks. "What if the bad men come here?"

"Bad men?" Mrs. Mallory asked, her brow wrinkling with confusion and uneasiness.

Josie shrugged off the question. "He must have had a bad dream."

If only that had been all it was...

Just a bad dream.

The little boy vehemently shook his head. "The bad men were real and had guns. They were shootin' at us and then there was a big bang!"

Josie shook her head, too, trying to quiet the boy's fears and Mrs. Mallory's. "It must have been quite the dream," she said, "and his imagination is so vivid."

Mrs. Mallory glanced from the boy to Josie and back. "He does have quite the imagination," she agreed, his story, although true, too fanciful for the older woman to believe. "He's a very creative boy. Did you watch a scary movie with him last night— something that brought on such a horrible dream?"

"No," Josie replied. She touched her little boy's trembling chin. "You have no reason to be afraid," she told him. "You're perfectly safe here."

Not buying her assurances in the least, CJ shook his head and wriggled out of Mrs. Mallory's arms. "I need my daddy to p'tect me."

Brendan had gone from bad man to hero for his son. He needed to know that; hopefully he was alive for her to share that news with him. She needed to get to her house. If it had blown up, she would have heard the explosion—or at least the fire trucks.

He had to be okay....

Josie knelt in front of her son and met his gaze. "I

am going to go get your daddy," she promised, "and he will come back here with me to get you, okay?"

"I can get Daddy, too," he said, throwing his arms around her neck to cling to her.

Her heart broke, but she forced herself to tug him off and stand up. He used to cling to her like this every morning when she'd first started bringing him to Mrs. Mallory, but today was the first time he'd had a reason for his fears. Not only because of the night he'd had, but also because she might not be able to come back— if she walked into the same trap his father might have. But then his godmother would take him....

Charlotte. She wouldn't have endangered them. Brendan must have had another reason for not returning to the SUV. Maybe that injury to his head was more severe than he'd led her to believe.

"No, honey," she said, and it physically hurt her, tightened her stomach into knots, to deny his fervent request. The timid boy asked her for so little that she hated telling him no. "I have to talk to Daddy alone first, and then we'll come get you."

Mrs. Mallory had always helped Josie escape before when her son was determined to cling. But now the older woman just stood in the foyer, her jaw hanging open in shock. As Josie stared at her, she pulled herself together. But curiosity obviously overwhelmed her. "His—his father? You've never mentioned him before."

With good reason. She had thought he wanted her dead. "We haven't been in contact in years," she honestly replied.

"But he's here?"

She nodded. "At my house."

Or so she hoped. Maybe he'd come back to where

he'd parked the SUV and found her gone. What would he think? That she'd tricked him again?

Hopefully she wasn't the one who'd been tricked. Hopefully he wasn't right about Charlotte.

"I—I have to go," she said. It had been too long. Now that she'd stood up, CJ was clinging to her legs.

Finally Mrs. Mallory stepped in and pried the sniffling child off her.

"I'll be back," she promised her son.

"With Daddy?"

She hoped so. But when she parked in the alley behind her house moments later, her hope waned. She hadn't seen him walking along the street. And while the house wasn't in pieces or on fire, it looked deserted.

She opened the driver's door and stepped out into the eerie quiet. Her neighbors would have already left for work, their kids for school. Josie was rarely home this time of day during the week. Maybe that was why it felt so strange to walk up to her own back door.

The glass in the window of the door was shattered. Of course, since Brendan had left her keys in the car, he would have had to break in to gain entrance. She was surprised he would have done it with such force, though, since the wooden panes were broken and the glass shattered as if it had exploded.

She sucked in a breath of fear. But she smelled no telltale odor of gas or smoke. The glass may have exploded, but a bomb had not.

Could a gunshot have broken the window?

If so, her neighbors would have called the police. There would have been officers at her home, crime scene tape blocking it off from the street. But there was nothing but a light breeze blowing through her broken window and rattling the blind inside.

The blind was broken, like the panes and the glass. Had Brendan slammed his fist through it? Or had someone else?

Gathering all her courage, she opened that door and stepped inside the small back porch. Glass crunched beneath her feet, crushed between the soles of her shoes and the slate floor. As she passed the washer and dryer on her way to the kitchen, she noticed a brick and crumpled paper sitting atop the washer.

Someone had thrown a brick through her window? Brendan?

Or was he the one who'd found it and picked it up? She suspected the latter, since there had obviously been a note secured to the brick with a rubber band. The broken band lay beside the brick and the crumpled paper.

She picked up the note and shivered with fear as she read the words: *You should have been the one who died.*

Oh, God. She was too late. Brendan had walked into a trap meant for her.

Chapter Thirteen

The scream startled Brendan, chilling his blood. He'd lost all sense of time and place. How long ago had he left Josie and their son? Had someone found them?

He'd left them alone and defenseless but for the gun he'd given Josie. Had she even had any bullets left?

He reached for the weapon at his back, pulling the gun from under his jacket. Then he crept up the stairs from the room he'd found in the basement, the one that had answered all the questions he'd had about ever trusting Josie Jessup.

The old steps creaked beneath his weight, giving away his presence. A shadow stood at the top of the stairwell, blocking Brendan's escape. The dim bulb swinging overhead glinted off the metal of the gun the shadow held, the barrel pointed at Brendan. He lifted his gun and aimed. But then he noticed the hair and the figure. "Josie!"

"Brendan? You're alive!" She launched herself at him, nearly knocking him off the stairs. "I thought you were dead!"

He caught himself against the brick wall at his back. "Now you know how it feels," he murmured. Despite his bitterness, his arms closed around her, holding her against him.

Her heart pounded madly. "I was so worried about you. You didn't come back to the car and then I found that note."

"You thought that note referred to me?"

She nodded.

"As you can see, I'm alive," he said. "So who does it refer to?"

She gasped as that guilt flashed across her face again.

And he remembered the sign. "Michael?"

"Yes," she miserably replied. "Some people blame me for his death."

"Did you kill him?"

She gasped again in shock and outrage. "No. I would never…"

"It's not a good feeling to have people thinking you're a killer," he remarked.

Her brow furrowed with confusion as he set her away from him. "Where have you been all this time?" she asked. As he turned and headed back down the steps, she followed him. "You've been down here?" Then as she realized exactly where he'd been, she ran ahead of him and tried blocking the doorway to her den.

Bookshelves lined knotty pine walls. But it wasn't there he'd found what he'd spent the past four years looking for.

"You broke into my filing cabinet!" she said.

He could have lied and blamed it on whoever had thrown the brick through her window. But that person would have had no interest in what he'd discovered. So he just shrugged.

"You had no right!" she said, as she hurried over to where he'd spread the files across her desk.

"I think I have more right to those records than you do," he pointed out. "They're all about me."

She trembled as she shoved the papers back into folders. "But you shouldn't have seen them."

"That's what you were working on when we were together," he said, his gut aching as it had when he'd found the folders. If the drawer hadn't been locked, he probably wouldn't have bothered to jimmy it open. But he'd wanted to know all her secrets so that he might figure out who was trying to kill her. "You thought I killed my own father? That's the story you were after when you came after me."

She released a shuddery sigh. "That was a lifetime ago."

"But you're still a reporter."

She shook her head. "No."

"You teach journalism," he said, gesturing toward a framed award that sat among the books on the shelves of the den. She had given up so much of her old life, except for that. No matter where she was or what she was calling herself, she was still a journalist.

"I teach," she said, her tone rueful, "because I can't *do*."

"Because you can't give it up." Not for him. Not even for their son.

"I had to give up everything," she said. "My home. My family."

Family.

"Where's CJ?" he asked, glancing around the shadows. She'd been alone on the stairs. Where had she stashed their child this time?

"He's at his sitter's," she said. "He's safe."

"Are you sure?" He never should have let the boy out of his sight.

"I can trust the people here."

Skeptical, he snorted. "She wouldn't have thrown the brick?"

"Absolutely not," she said. "It must have been one of my other students. Or one of Michael's friends."

"What happened to Michael?"

Sadness dimmed her eyes and filled them with tears. "He was killed pursuing a story."

He touched his fingers to the scratch on his temple. It didn't sting anymore; it throbbed, the intensity of it increasing with his confusion and frustration. "How could you be responsible for that?"

Her eyes glistened with moisture. "It was a story I suggested that he cover." She blinked back the tears. "But that brick—that has nothing to do with what happened in Chicago. Nobody here knows who I really am. Nobody here would have tried to kill me."

"Just scare you," he said. But the brick and the note were nothing in comparison to gunfire and explosions. "You should be scared," he said. He reached out and jerked one of the folders from her hand. "This story could have gotten *you* killed."

She sucked in a quivering breath. "It almost did. It is why someone tried to kill me four years ago."

"Someone," he agreed. And now he knew who. "But not me."

She gestured toward those folders. "But you see why I suspected you. All the people I talked to named you as your father's killer."

People he should have been able to trust—men who'd worked with his father since they were kids selling drugs for Brendan's grandfather. And his stepmother. When his father had first married her, she had pretended to care about her husband's motherless son. But when Brendan had returned to claim the inheritance Margaret O'Hannigan thought should have been hers, she'd stopped pretending.

Josie continued, "In all the conversations I overheard while hanging out with you at O'Hannigan's, only one suspect was ever named in his murder."

"Me." Did she still suspect him?

"I was wrong," she admitted, but then defended herself. "But I didn't know you very well then. You were so secretive and you never answered my questions."

She didn't know him very well now, either. But it was obvious she couldn't stop being a journalist, so he couldn't trust her with the truth. He couldn't tell her who he really was, but he could tell her something about himself.

"We wanted the same thing, you know," he told her.

"We did?" she asked, the skepticism all hers now.

"I didn't want an award-winning exposé," he clarified. "But I wanted the truth."

She nodded. "That's why I never printed anything. I had no confirmation. No proof. I could have written an exposé. But I wanted the truth."

And that was the one thing that set her apart from the other reporters who'd done stories about him over the past four years. She wouldn't print the unsubstantiated rumors other journalists would. She'd wanted proof. She just hadn't recognized it when she'd found it.

"I want to know who killed him, too," he said. "I came back to that *life* because I wanted justice for my father." After years of trying to bring the man to justice, it was ironic that Brendan had spent the past four years trying to get justice for his father—for his cold-blooded murder.

"You spent a lot of time reading through everything," she said, staring down at the desk he'd messed up. "Did you find anything I missed?"

Because he didn't want to lie outright to her, he replied, "You weren't the only one who must have gone through those papers. If there'd been something in there, one of the marshals would have found it."

"Nobody else has ever seen this stuff," she admitted.

The pounding in his head increased. If anyone familiar with his father's murder case had looked at her records, they would have figured it out. They would have recognized that one of her sources knew too much about the murder scene, things that only the killer would have known. She never would have had to go into hiding, never would have had to keep his child from him. "Why the hell not?"

She lifted her chin with pride. "My dad taught me young to respect the code."

"What code?"

"The journalist code," she said. "A true journalist *never* reveals a source."

Ignoring the pain, he shook his head with disgust. "After the attempts on your life, I think Stanley Jessup would have understood."

She chuckled. "You don't know my dad."

"No," he said, "you never introduced me. I was your dirty little secret."

"He would have been mad," she admitted. "He wouldn't have wanted me anywhere near you, given your reputation."

"Good," Brendan said. He'd worried that the man had put her up to it, to getting close to him for a story.

"And if he cared that much for your safety, he would have understood you breaking the code."

She nodded. "Probably. But I didn't think so back then. Back then, I figured he would have been happier for me to die than reveal a source."

"Josie!" He reached for her, to offer assurance. He knew what it was like to feel like a disappointment to one's father. But when his arms closed around her, he wanted to offer more than sympathy. He wanted her... as he always did.

"But I realized that he wouldn't have cared about the code. He would have cared only about keeping me safe when I had CJ," she said. "CJ!"

She said his name with guilt and alarm, as if something bad had happened to their child.

"What? What about CJ?"

PULLING HIM OFF her, leaving him, had killed her earlier. She hated disappointing her child. So she'd kept her promise and had brought Brendan with her to pick up their son.

And for the entire day they had acted like a normal family. CJ had proudly showed Brendan all his toys and books, which the rumored mob boss had patiently played with and read to the three-year-old boy. Brendan had also looked through all the photos of their son, seeing in pictures every milestone that had been stolen from him.

Through no fault of his own. It was her fault for not trusting him. But she'd felt then that he had been keeping secrets from her. And she had imagined the worst.

As Brendan, with CJ sitting on his lap, continued to flip through the photo albums, she felt every emotion that flickered across his handsome face, the loss, the regret and the awe. He loved their son.

Could he ever love her?

Or had her lies and mistrust destroyed whatever he might have been able to feel for her? If only she'd known then what that damn story would wind up costing her...

The only man she would ever love.

He glanced up and caught her watching them, and his beautiful eyes darkened. With anger? Was he mad at her?

She couldn't blame him. She was mad at herself for all that she had denied him and her son. So today she'd tried making it up to them. She'd made all CJ's favorite foods, played all his favorite games, and she'd pretended that last night had never happened.

The gunfire. The explosion.

She was actually almost able to forget those. It was making love with Brendan that wouldn't leave her mind. She could almost feel his lips on hers, his hands on her body.

Feel him inside her...

She shivered.

"Why don't you take a shower," he said. "Warm up."

God, did she still look like hell?

"It's getting late," she said. "CJ should go to bed, too." The little boy had already had his bath. Brendan had helped give it to him. His rolled-up shirtsleeves were still damp from playing with the ducks and boats in the tub.

"I'll put him to bed," Brendan offered, as if he didn't want to waste a minute of the time he had with his son.

She had longed to clean up, so she agreed with a silent nod. But knowing that her little boy had to be tired, she leaned down to press a kiss to his forehead. "Good night, sweetheart."

Over the red curls of their son, she met Brendan's gaze. His eyes were dark, but not with anger. At least not anger she felt was directed at her. But he was intense, on edge.

As if he were biding his time…

To leave? Was his desire to tuck CJ in so that he could say goodbye?

THE HOUSE WAS small, but it had two bathrooms. So while she was soaking in the tub in the one off her bedroom, he'd used the small shower in the hall bathroom. But when he pushed open the steamed-up door, she was standing there—wrapped in a towel, waiting for him.

His pulse quickened, and his body hardened with desire. Her gaze flicked down him and then up again, her pupils wide with longing.

"Guess I should have locked the door," he remarked even as he reached for her. He slid his fingers between her breasts, pulling loose the ends of the towel she'd tucked in her cleavage, and then he dragged the towel off her damp body. He pulled the thick terry cloth across his own wet skin as she squeaked in protest.

"Hey!"

"Oh, I thought you'd meant to bring me a towel, like a good hostess." All day she'd played the perfect host, making sure that he and CJ had everything they'd needed. As if she'd felt guilty for keeping them apart.

Was that why she was here now? Out of guilt?

He wanted her, but not that way. God, he wanted her though. She was so damn beautiful, her silky skin flushed from her bath, her curves so full and soft.

He curled his hands into fists so that he wouldn't

reach for her. He had to know first. "Why are you here?"

"Why are you?" she asked. "I figured when I got out of my bath that I would find you gone."

He'd thought about it. But he'd had trouble getting CJ to keep his eyes closed. Every time he'd thought he could leave the little boy's bedside, CJ had dragged his lids up again and asked for Daddy.

Brendan's heart clutched with emotion: love like he'd never known. He'd felt a responsibility to his father to find his killer. But the responsibility he felt to CJ was far greater, because the kid needed and deserved him more. Brendan had to keep the little boy safe—even if he had to give up his own life.

"Why would you think that I would be gone?" he asked. Had becoming a mother given her new instincts? Psychic powers?

"I can feel it," she said. "Your anxiousness. Your edginess."

"You make me anxious," he said. "Edgy…"

She sucked in a shaky breath. And despite the warmth of the steamy shower, her nipples peaked, as if pouting for his touch. He wanted to oblige.

"You make me anxious," she said, "that you're going to sneak out."

"Why would I do that?"

"Because you learned something from going through my files earlier," she said, and her eyes narrowed with suspicion.

"Are you ever not suspicious of me?" he asked, even though this time he couldn't deny that she had reason to be. She'd nearly lost her life, several times, because of him. He wouldn't let her put herself in danger again.

She had so much more to lose now than she'd been forced to give up before.

"I wouldn't be," she replied, "if I ever felt like you were being completely honest with me. But there are always these secrets between us."

"You've kept secrets, too," he reminded her. "One of them is sleeping in the other room."

As if remembering that their son was close, she grabbed a towel from the rack behind her and wrapped it around her naked body.

He sighed his disappointment and hooked the towel he'd stolen from her around his waist. He'd wanted to make love with her again. He'd needed to make love with her again...before he left her.

But she opened the door first as if unable to bear the heat of the bathroom any longer. He followed her down the hall to her bedroom. Like the rest of the house, she'd decorated it warmly. The kitchen was sunny-yellow, the living room orange and her bedroom was a deep red. Like the passion that always burned between them.

"The difference between us," she said, "is that I don't have any more secrets."

He closed the door behind his back before crossing the room and grabbing her towel again. "No, no more secrets."

"You can't say the same," she accused him.

"I know how you feel," he said. "How you taste..."

And he leaned down to kiss her lips. Hers clung to his. And her fingers skimmed over his chest. She wanted him, too.

He slid his mouth across her cheek and down her neck to her shoulder. She shivered in reaction and moaned his name. "Your skin is so warm," he murmured. "So silky."

He skimmed his palms down her back, along the curve of her spine to the rounded swells of her butt. She'd been sexy before, but thin with sharp curves. Now she was more rounded. Soft and so damn sexy that just touching her tried his control.

He had to taste her, too. He gently pushed her down onto the bed. He kissed his way down her body, from her shoulder, over the curve of her breasts. He sucked a taut nipple between his lips and teased it with the tip of his tongue.

She squirmed beneath him, touching him everywhere she could reach. His back. His butt…

He swallowed a groan as the tension built inside him. Another part of him other than his head throbbed and ached, rubbing against her and begging for release.

But he denied his own pleasure to prolong hers. He moved from her breasts, over the soft curve of her stomach to that apex of curls. He teased with his tongue, sliding it in and out of her.

She clutched at his back and then his hair. She arched and wriggled and moaned. And then she came—shattering with ecstasy.

While she was still wet and pulsing, he thrust inside her. And her inner muscles clutched at him, pulling him deeper. She wrapped her legs and arms around him and met each of his thrusts.

Their mouths mated, their kisses frantic, lips clinging, tongue sliding over tongue. He didn't even need to touch her before she shattered again. He thrust once more and joined her in madness—unable to breathe, unable to think…

He could only feel. Pleasure. And love.

He loved her. That was why he had to make certain she would never be in danger again because of him. If he had to give up his life for hers and their son's, he would do it willingly.

Chapter Fourteen

Her body ached. Not from the explosion or even from running from gunmen. Her body ached from making love. Josie smiled and rolled over, reaching across the bed. The sheets were still warm, tangled and scented with their lovemaking. He'd made love to her again and again until she'd fallen into an exhausted slumber.

And she realized why when she jerked awake to an empty bed. An empty room. He'd left her. She didn't need to search her house to confirm that he was gone. But she pulled on a robe and checked CJ's room before she looked through the rest of the house.

Her son slept peacefully, the streetlamp casting light through his bedroom window. It made his red curls glow like fire, reminding her of the explosion.

And she hurried up her search, running through the house before reaching out over the basement stairwell to jerk down the pull chain on the dangling bulb. It swung out over the steps, the light dancing around her as she hurried down to her den. He wasn't there and neither were her folders.

He had found something in them. What?

What had she had?

Notes she'd taken from the conversations she'd overheard in the bar and from informal interviews she'd done with other members of the O'Hannigan family. News clippings from other reporters who'd covered the story. Sloppily. They hadn't dug nearly as deep as she had. A copy of the case file from his father's murder, which she'd bought off a cop on the force. Brendan wasn't wrong that many people had a price. They could be bought.

But not Charlotte.

Too bad the former U.S. marshal wasn't close enough to help her now. Maybe Josie wasn't close enough, either—to stop Brendan from doing what she was afraid he was about to do: either confront or kill his father's murderer.

"But who? Who is it?" she murmured to herself.

She'd gone through the folders so many times that she pretty much had the contents memorized. Brendan had figured it out; so could she. But she couldn't let him keep his head start on her. She had to catch up with him.

No doubt he had taken her SUV. But she had another car parked in the garage off the alley, a rattletrap Volkswagen convertible. It wasn't pretty, but mechanically it should be sound enough to get her back to Chicago. She had bought the car from a student desperate to sell it for money to buy textbooks.

She had never had to struggle for cash as her community college students did. Her father had given her everything she'd ever wanted.

Brendan's father had not done the same for him. In fact, if rumors could ever be believed, Dennis O'Hannigan had taken away the one thing—the one person—who had mattered most to Brendan: his mother.

Why would he want to avenge the man's death? Why would he care enough to get justice for him?

Was it a code? Like the one her father had taught her. She shrugged off her concerns for now. She had to wake CJ and take him over to Mrs. Mallory's.

The little boy murmured in protest as she lifted him from his bed. "C'mon, sweetheart," she said. "I need to take you to Mrs. M's."

He shook his head. "I don't wanna go. Gotta p'tect you like Daddy said."

She tensed. "Daddy told you to protect me?"

"Uh-huh," CJ murmured. "He's gonna get rid of a bad person and then he'll come home to us."

The words her sleepy son uttered had everything falling into place for Josie. Brendan may not have trusted her enough to tell her the truth. But he had inadvertently told their son.

BRENDAN WASN'T SURE who he could trust, especially now that he knew who'd killed his father. But he knew that Josie had at least one person she could trust—besides himself.

Charlotte Green's outraged gasp rattled the phone. "You thought I might have given up her location?"

He pressed his fingers to that scratch on his head. If the bullet hadn't just grazed him…

No, he wouldn't let himself think about what might have happened to Josie and his son. She'd had the gun though—she would have defended herself and their child.

He glanced around the inside of the surveillance van, which was filled with equipment and people—people he wasn't sure he should have trusted despite their federal clearances. If U.S. marshals could be bought, so could FBI agents. He lowered his voice. "After gunmen tracked us down at my safe house and tried to kill us…"

"I didn't even know where you were when you called me, and if I had," she said, her voice chilly with offended pride, "I sure as well wouldn't have sent gunmen after you and Josie and my godson."

He still wasn't so sure about that. But, he realized, she hadn't told anyone where she'd relocated Josie. Why keep that secret and reveal anything else?

"You must have been followed," she said.

He'd thought about that but rejected the notion. "No. Nobody followed us that night."

"Maybe another night then," she suggested. "Someone must have figured out where you would take her."

The only people who knew about the safe house were fellow FBI agents. He glanced around the van, wondering if one of them had betrayed him, if one of them had been bought like Charlotte's former partner had been bought and like he'd thought she might have been. "You didn't trace the call?"

"No."

He snorted in derision. "I thought you were being honest with me. That's why I trusted you."

More than he trusted the crew he'd handpicked. The other men messed with the equipment, setting up mikes and cameras, and he watched them—checking to see if anyone had pulled out a phone as he had. But then if they were tipping off someone, they could have made that call already, before they'd joined him.

"But you must have a GPS on that phone you gave her," he continued, calling her on her lie. "You must have some way to keep tabs on her."

She chuckled. "Okay, maybe I do."

That was why he'd left Josie the phone. "That's what I thought."

"Until recently she was easy to track," Charlotte said. "She was at home or the college."

"Teaching journalism," he remarked. "That's why you kept my secret from her. You realized that I had reason to be cautious with her. That no matter how much you changed her appearance or her identity, she was still a reporter."

"A teacher," Charlotte corrected him.

He snorted again. "Of journalism." And she'd still had the inclination to seek out dangerous stories. For her, there was no story more dangerous than this one. He had to make certain she was far away from him.

"Use your GPS," he ordered, "and tell me where she is now." Hopefully still at home, asleep in the bed he'd struggled to leave. He had wanted to hold her all night; he'd wanted to hold her forever.

Some strange noise emanated from the phone.

"Charlotte?"

"She's on the move."

"But I took her car." She must have borrowed a neighbor's or maybe Mrs. Mallory's. Hopefully, she'd left their son with his babysitter.

"The Volkswagen, too?"

"I didn't know she had another." As modestly as she'd been living in that small, outdated house, he hadn't considered she'd had the extra money for another car.

Charlotte sighed. "I'm surprised that clunker was up to the trip."

"Trip?"

"She's in Chicago."

"Damn it," he cursed at her. "I could have used you

here. I'm surprised you didn't come to help protect her. She thinks you're her friend."

"I am."

"You're also a princess. What is it? Couldn't spare the time from waving at adoring crowds?"

"I'm also pregnant," she said, and there was that sound again. "And currently in labor…since last night. Or I would have come. I would have sent someone I trusted, but they refused to leave me."

Brendan flinched at his insensitivity.

"So like you asked me to, I trusted you," she said. "I thought if anyone would keep Josie safe, it would be the man who loves her."

"I'm trying," he said. And the best way to do that was to remove the threat against her.

He glanced at the monitors flanking one side of the surveillance van. One of the cameras caught a vehicle careening down the street, right toward the estate they were watching on the outskirts of Chicago.

For all the rust holes, he couldn't tell what color the vehicle was. "Her second car," he said. "Is it an old convertible Cabriolet?" Even though the top was currently up, it looked so frayed that there were probably holes in it, too.

"Yes," Charlotte said.

"I have to go," he said, clicking off the cell. But it wasn't just the call he had to abort. He had to stop the whole operation.

"Block the driveway!" he yelled at one of the men wearing a headset. That agent could communicate with the agents outside the van. But he only stared blankly at Brendan, as if unable to comprehend what he was saying. "Stop the car," he explained. "Don't let her get to the house."

"From the way you're acting, I'm guessing that's the reporter you dated," another of the agents inside the van addressed Brendan. He must have been eavesdropping on his conversation with Charlotte. Or he'd tapped into it. "The one you just discovered was put into witness protection and that she had the evidence all this time?"

This agent was Brendan's superior in ranking, and even though he had worked with him for years—four years on this assignment alone—he didn't know him well enough to know about his character.

Could he be trusted?

Could any of them, inside the van or out?

His blood chilled in his veins, and he shook his head, disgusted with himself for giving away Josie's identity so easily. All of his fellow agents had been well aware of how he'd felt about Josie Jessup.

"It isn't?" the agent asked.

"No, it's her," he admitted. "And that's why we have to stop her." Before she confronted face-to-face the person who'd tried to kill her.

The supervising agent shook his head, stopping the man with the headset from making the call to stop her. So Brendan took it upon himself and reached for the handle of the van's sliding door. But strong hands caught him, holding him back and pinning his arms behind him.

Damn it.

He should have followed his instincts to trust no one. He should have done it alone. But he'd wanted to go through the right channels—had wanted true justice, not vigilante justice. But maybe with people as powerful as these, with people who could buy off police officers and federal agents, the only justice was vigilante.

HE WAS GOING TO kill her.

Josie had to stop him—had to stop Brendan from doing something he would live to regret. Taking justice into his own hands would take away the chance for him to have a real relationship with his son.

And her?

She didn't expect him to forgive her for thinking he was a killer. She didn't expect him to trust her, especially after she'd come here. But she had to stop him.

She hadn't seen her white SUV along the street or along the long driveway leading up to the house. But that didn't mean he hadn't exchanged it for one of those she had seen. The house, a brick Tudor, looked eerily similar to Brendan's, just on a smaller scale. Like a model of the original O'Hannigan home.

Brendan had to be here. Unless it was already done....

Was she was too late? Had he already taken his justice and left?

The gates stood open, making it easy for her to drive through and pull her Volkswagen up to the house. But she hadn't even put it in Park before someone was pulling open her door and dragging her from behind the steering wheel. She had no time to reach inside her bag and pull out the gun.

Strong hands held tightly to her arms, shoving her up the brick walk to the front door. It stood open, a woman standing in the doorway as if she'd been expecting her.

Yet she acted puzzled, her brow furrowed as if she was trying to place Josie. Of course, Josie didn't look the same as she had when she'd informally interviewed Margaret O'Hannigan four years ago. Back then the woman had believed Josie was just her stepson's girlfriend. And since they'd only met a few times, it was no wonder she wouldn't as easily see through Josie's disguise as Brendan had.

But Margaret must have realized she'd given herself up during one of their conversations. That was why Margaret had tried to kill Josie.

While Josie had changed much over the past few years, this woman hadn't changed at all. She was still beautiful—her face smooth of wrinkles and ageless. Her hair was rich and dark and devoid of any hint of gray despite the fact that she had to be well into her fifties. She was still trim and tiny. Her beauty and fragile build might have been what had fooled Josie into excluding her as a suspect in her husband's murder.

But now she detected a strength and viciousness about the woman as she stared at Josie, her dark eyes cold and emotionless. "Who the hell are you?" she demanded.

"Josie Jessup," she replied honestly. There was no point clinging to an identity that had already been blown.

"Josie Jessup? I thought you were dead," the woman remarked.

Josie had thought the same of her. That Brendan might have killed her by now.

"Are you responsible for this?" Margaret asked, gesturing toward the open gates and the dark house. An alarm sounded from within, an insistent beeping that must have driven her to the door. "Did you disable the security system, forcing open the gates and unlocking the doors?"

Brendan must have. He was here then. Somewhere. Josie wasn't too late.

"Search her car," Margaret ordered the man who'd held her arms.

Josie stumbled forward as he released her. But the woman didn't step back, didn't allow Josie inside her house.

"I wouldn't know how to disable a security system," Josie assured her. "I am no criminal mastermind."

"No, you're a reporter," Margaret said. "That was why you were always asking all those questions."

"And you were always eager to answer them," Josie reminded her. Too eager, since she hadn't realized she'd given herself away. But then neither had Josie. She still wasn't sure exactly what it was in those folders that had convinced Brendan of the woman's guilt. "You were eager to point the blame at your stepson."

"A man shouldn't benefit from a murder he committed," she said, stubbornly clinging to her lies.

"Brendan didn't kill his father," Josie said, defending the man she loved.

Margaret smiled, but her eyes remained cold. "You weren't so convinced back then. You suspected him just like everyone else."

"And just like everyone else, I was wrong," Josie admitted. "But you knew that."

The woman tensed and stepped out from the doorway. She held a gun in her hand.

For protection? Because of the security breach? Or because someone had tipped her off that either Brendan or Josie was coming to confront her?

"How would I know something that the authorities did not?" Margaret asked, but a small smile lifted her thin lips. "They all believed Brendan responsible, as well."

"But they could never find proof."

"Because he was clever."

"Because he was innocent."

The woman laughed. "You loved him."

It wasn't a question, so Josie didn't reply. Or deny what was probably pathetically obvious to everyone but Brendan.

"That's a pity," the woman commiserated. "It's not easy to love an O'Hannigan. At least you don't need to worry about that anymore."

"I don't?" Josie asked.

"Brendan is dead."

Pain clutched her heart, hurting her as much as if the woman had fired a bullet into her heart. He'd already been here. And gone.

"You didn't know?" Margaret asked. "Some journalist you are. How did you miss the reports?"

Had his death already made the news? The Volkswagen had no radio—just a hole in the dash where one had once been. The kid who'd sold her the auto had been willing to part with his car but not his sound system.

Margaret sighed regretfully. "And it was such a beautiful estate. I'd hoped to return there one day."

"The house?"

"It blew up…with Brendan inside." Margaret shook her head. "Such a loss." With a nasty smile, she clarified, "The house, not Brendan."

The explosion. She was talking about the explosion. Brendan wasn't dead. Relief eased the horrible tightness in Josie's chest, but the sigh she uttered was of disgust with the woman. "How can you be so…"

"Practical?" Margaret asked. "It's so much better than being a romantic fool."

Josie hadn't been a fool for being romantic; she'd been a fool for doubting Brendan. Then. And maybe now.

If he'd intended to kill his stepmother, wouldn't he have already been here? Where was he?

"You're better off," Margaret assured her. "You were stupid to fall for him."

"You didn't love your husband?" Josie asked. That would explain how she'd killed him in cold blood.

She chuckled. "My mama always told me that it was easier to love a rich man than a poor man. My mama had never met Dennis O'Hannigan." She shuddered but her grip stayed steady on the gun. "You were lucky to get away from his son."

"Brendan is—was—" she corrected herself. It was smarter to let the woman think the explosion she'd ordered had worked. "He was nothing like his father."

"You don't believe that or you wouldn't have gone into hiding," Margaret remarked. "You even changed your hair and your face. You must have really been afraid of him."

She had spent almost four years being afraid of the wrong person.

"Were you afraid of his father?" Josie asked.

Margaret shrugged her delicate shoulders. "A person would have been crazy to *not* be afraid of Dennis."

Dennis wasn't the only O'Hannigan capable of inspiring fear. Neither was Brendan.

Despite her small stature, Margaret O'Hannigan was an intimidating woman.

So Josie should have held her tongue. She should have stopped asking her questions. But maybe Brendan was right—maybe she wasn't capable of *not* being a journalist. Because she had to know...

Even if the question cost her everything, she had to ask, "Is that why you killed him?"

Chapter Fifteen

Brendan fought against the men holding him. He shoved back with his body and his head. He knocked the back of his skull against one man's nose, dropping him to the floor while the other stumbled into the equipment. Then he whipped a gun from his holster and whirled to confront his attackers.

Men he had hoped he could trust: fellow FBI agents.

"I should have known," he berated himself. "I should have known the leak was inside the Bureau. I should have known there was no one I could trust."

Special Agent Martinez, the man supervising the assignment, calmly stared down the barrel of Brendan's gun. "I've heard about this happening to agents like you, ones who've been undercover more than they've been out. Ones who get so paranoid of the lives they're living that they lose their grasp on reality. On sanity. You're losing it, O'Hannigan."

"No, we're losing *her*," Brendan said, as one of the monitors showed Josie walking inside the house with a killer. Margaret O'Hannigan held a gun, too, pointed at the woman he loved.

"We've got the house wired," Martinez reminded him. "We're going to hear everything that they say."

"But the plan was for *me* to get her to talk," he said and lowered the gun to his side. He wasn't going to use it. Yet…

Martinez nodded in agreement. "But once she sees you're alive, you wouldn't get anything out of her."

"Neither will Josie," he argued.

"Josie Jessup is a reporter." Martinez was the one who'd confirmed Brendan's suspicions about it, who'd tracked her back to the stories written under the pseudonym of Jess Ley. "A damn good one. She fooled you four years ago."

And allowing himself to be deceived and distracted had nearly gotten Brendan thrown off the case. But because he'd inherited his father's business, he had been the only one capable of getting inside the organization and taking it apart, as the FBI had been trying to do for years.

"She won't fool Margaret." Because Margaret had fooled them all for years. Even his father.

Martinez shook his head. "She's Stanley Jessup's daughter. She has a way of making people talk. She knows what buttons to push, what questions to ask."

That was what Brendan was afraid of—that she'd push the wrong buttons. "If Margaret admits anything to her, it's only because she intends to kill her."

"Then we'll go in," Martinez assured him. "The evidence you found got us the federal warrants for the surveillance. But there isn't enough for an arrest. We need a confession. You were the one who pointed that out."

And he'd intended to get the confession himself. He hadn't intended to use Josie—to put her in danger. Their son needed his mother; Brendan needed her, too.

On the surveillance monitors, one of Margaret's

bodyguards walked into the house, something swinging from the hand that wasn't holding a gun.

"We won't get there fast enough to save her," Brendan said, as foreboding and dread clutched his heart. The van was parked outside the gates. Even though they were open, thanks to the security system being dismantled, they were still too far down the driveway.

"There are guys closer," Martinez reminded him.

But were they guys he could trust? Could he really trust anyone?

SHE SHOULD HAVE trusted Brendan. Just because he'd discovered the identity of his father's killer didn't mean he was going to avenge the man's death.

But she'd thought the worst of him again. And she'd worried that CJ would lose his father before he ever got a chance to really know him. Now a gun was pointed at her, and the risk was greater that CJ would lose his mother. At least he had his godmother; Charlotte would take him. She would protect him as Josie had failed to do.

With the lights off and the draperies pulled, it was dark inside the house—nearly as dark as if night had fallen already. Except a little sliver of sunlight sneaked through a crack in the drapes and glinted off the metal of Margaret O'Hannigan's gun.

She looked much more comfortable holding a weapon than Josie was. Maybe she should reach for hers. Her purse was on the hardwood floor next to where Margaret had pushed her down onto the couch. Even the inside of the home was a replica of Dennis O'Hanningan's.

"Are you insinuating that I killed my husband? What

the hell are you talking about?" the older woman demanded to know.

"The truth." A concept that Josie suspected Margaret O'Hannigan was not all that familiar with. "And I'm not insinuating. I'm flat-out saying that you're the one. You killed Brendan's father."

"How dare you accuse me of killing my husband!" she exclaimed, clearly offended, probably not because Josie thought her capable of murder but because she hadn't gotten away with it.

Hell, she would still probably get away with it. Josie glanced down at her bag again. She needed to grab her gun, needed to defend herself. But then it was no longer just the two of them.

Heavy footsteps echoed on the hardwood flooring. "There was nothing in her car," the man who had dragged Josie from the Volkswagen informed his boss as he joined them inside the house. "But this."

Josie turned to see CJ's booster seat dangling from his hand.

"You have a child?" Margaret asked.

She could have lied, claimed she'd borrowed a friend's car. But she was curious. Would Margaret spare her because she was a mother? "Why does it matter that I have a son?"

"How old is he?" Margaret asked.

"Three." Too young to lose his mother, especially as she'd been the only parent he'd ever known until a day ago.

Margaret shook her head. "No. No. No..."

"It's okay," Josie said. "You can let me go. I don't really know anything. I have no proof that you killed Dennis O'Hannigan."

The man glanced from her to Margaret and back.

Had he not worked for her back then? Had he not realized his employer was a killer?

Maybe he would protect her from the madwoman.

"You have something far worse," Margaret said. "You have Brendan O'Hannigan's son."

"Wh-what?"

"The last time I saw you, I suspected you were pregnant," Margaret admitted. "You were—" her mouth twisted into a derisive smirk "—glowing."

Josie hadn't even known she was pregnant then. She hadn't known until after her big fight with Brendan, until after she'd had the car accident when her brakes had given out and she'd been taken to the hospital. That was when she'd learned she carried his child.

"You—you don't know that my son is Brendan's," Josie pointed out.

"All I'll have to do is see a picture," she said. She pointed toward Josie's purse and ordered her employee, "Go through that."

He upended the contents of the bag, the gun dropping with a thud to the floor.

"You should have used that while you had the chance," Margaret said. "I didn't waste my chance."

"Are you talking about now?" Josie wondered. "Or when you shot your husband in the alley behind O'Hannigan's?" She suspected this woman was cold-blooded enough to have done it personally.

The man handed over Josie's wallet to his boss. The picture portfolio hung out of it, the series of photos a six-month progression of CJ from infancy to his birthday a couple of months ago. Usually people smiled when they saw the curly-haired boy. But his step-grandmother glowered.

"Damn it," Margaret cursed. "Damn those O'Hannigan eyes."

Josie could not deny her son's paternity. "Why do you care that Brendan has—had—a son?"

"Because I am not about to have another damn O'Hannigan heir come out of the woodwork again and claim what is rightfully mine," she replied angrily. "I worked damn hard for it. I earned it."

"So you didn't kill your husband because you were afraid of him. You killed him because you wanted his fortune," Josie mused aloud.

The woman's eyes glittered with rage and her face— once so beautiful—contorted into an ugly mask. "He was going to divorce me," she said, outraged at even the memory. "After all those years of putting up with his abuse, he was going to leave me. Claimed he never loved me."

"You never loved him, either," Josie pointed out.

"That was why it felt so damn good to pull the trigger," she admitted gleefully. "To see that look of surprise on his face as I shot him right in the chest. He had no idea who he was married to—had no idea that I could be as ruthless as he was. And that I was that good a shot."

So she had fired the gun herself. And apparently she'd taken great pleasure from it. Josie had no hope of this callous killer sparing her life.

Margaret chuckled wryly. "The coroner said the bullet hit him right in the heart. I was surprised because I didn't figure he had one."

"Then why did you marry him?"

"For the same reason I killed him—for the money," she freely admitted.

She stepped closer and pointed the barrel right at

Josie's head. "So your kid is damn well not going to come forward and claim it from me now."

Margaret thought Brendan was dead—that CJ was the only threat to her inheriting now. But if Brendan had really died, the estate would go to his heirs, not his stepmother. Then Josie remembered that Dennis O'Hannigan had had a codicil in his will that only an O'Hannigan would hold deed to the estate. Before Brendan had accepted his inheritance, he'd had to sign a document promising to leave it only to an O'Hannigan. Margaret must have thought she was the only one left.

"He's only three years old," Josie reminded her. "He's not going to take anything away from you."

"I didn't think Brendan would, either. After he ran away I thought he was never coming back." She sighed. "I thought his dad had made sure he could never come back, the same way that he had made sure Brendan's mother could never come back."

"You thought Dennis had killed him?"

"He should have," Margaret said. The woman wasn't just greedy; she was pure evil. "Then I wouldn't have had that nasty surprise."

She was going to have another one when she learned that once again Brendan wasn't dead. But if he wasn't… where was he? Shouldn't he have been here before now?

Could someone else have hurt him? Or maybe the authorities had brought him in for questioning about the explosion and the shootings at the hospital.…

Maybe if she bided her time…

But Margaret pressed the gun to Josie's temple as if ready to squeeze the trigger. The burly guard flinched as if he could feel Josie's pain. "Now you are going to tell me where you've left your brat so we can make sure I don't get another nasty surprise."

"He doesn't need your money," Josie pointed out. "He's a Jessup. My father has more money than CJ will ever be able to spend."

"CJ?"

Josie bit her tongue, appalled that she'd given away her son's name. Not that his first name alone would lead the woman to him.

"So where is CJ?"

"Someplace where you can't get to him," Josie assured herself more than the boy's step-grandmother. He was safe now, and Brendan would make certain he stayed that way. No matter what happened to her.

"You'll tell me," Margaret said as she slid her finger onto the trigger.

Uncaring that the barrel was pressed to her temple, Josie shook her head. "You might as well shoot me now, because I will never let you get to my son."

The trigger cocked, and Josie closed her eyes, waiting for it. Would it hurt? Or would it be over so quickly she wouldn't even realize it?

The gun barrel jerked back so abruptly that Josie's head jerked forward, too. "Help me persuade her," Margaret ordered her guard.

And Josie's head snapped again as the man slapped her. Her cheek stung and her eyes watered as pain overwhelmed her.

"Where is he?" Margaret asked.

Josie shook her head.

And the man slapped her again.

A cry slipped from her mouth as her lip cracked from the blow. Blood trickled from the stinging wound.

"I'm never going to tell you where my son is," she vowed. "I don't care how many times you hit me."

"I care."

Josie looked up to see Brendan saunter into the living room as nonchalantly as if he were just joining them for drinks. But instead of bringing a bottle of wine, he'd brought a gun—which he pointed directly at Margaret. Probably because she had whirled toward him with her weapon.

But her guard had pulled his gun, and he pressed the barrel to Josie's head. Brendan may have intended to rescue her, but Josie had a horrible feeling that they were about to make their son an orphan.

She should have thought it out before she'd chased after Brendan. She had been concerned about CJ losing his father, but now he might lose both his parents.

"I THOUGHT YOU were dead," Margaret said, slinging her words at him like an accusation.

"You keep making that mistake," Brendan said. "Guess that's just been wishful thinking on your part."

"I thought the explosion killed you."

"You were behind that?"

"I wanted you dead," she admitted, without actually claiming responsibility.

But she'd already confessed to enough to go away for a long time. Martinez had been right about Josie making her talk. Now that Josie had gotten what they'd wanted, he needed to get her to safety.

"I've wanted you dead for a long time," Margaret continued. "This time I'll personally make sure you're gone. You've disrupted my plans for the last time." She cocked her gun at him now. "Then we'll retrieve your son."

She gestured at Josie as if they were co-conspirators. Had she not heard anything Josie had said to her? Josie would die before she would give up her son's location. That was what a mother should be like. CJ was one lucky boy. And Brendan would make sure they were reunited soon.

But Margaret was not done. She was confessing to crimes she had yet to commit. Crimes that Brendan would make damn certain she never got the chance to commit. "And when I get rid of that kid, I'll be making damn sure there will be no more O'Hannigans."

"You're the one who'll be going away forever," Brendan warned her as he cocked his gun. But if he shot her, would the guy holding Josie surrender or kill her?

Chapter Sixteen

"Don't kill her," Josie implored Brendan. Maybe she had been right to be concerned that he would take matters into his own hands. But why had he taken so long to show up here? Where had he been?

Brendan narrowed his eyes as if he were still thinking about pulling the trigger, about taking a life. He could even excuse it as he had the others—that he'd done it to save another.

"Josie, I have to," he said, as if he'd been given no choice.

She had been thrilled to see him, thrilled that he might protect her from this madwoman. But she didn't want him becoming her—becoming a killer.

"You told me you wanted justice," she reminded him. "Not vengeance."

"He's a killer," Margaret said, spit flying from her mouth with disgust. "All O'Hannigans are killers. That's why it's best to get rid of the boy, too. Or he'll grow up just like Brendan has."

"Brendan isn't a killer," Josie told her—and him. "He came back for justice. He figured out you killed his father."

"How?" the woman arrogantly scoffed. "No one else has figured it out in four years."

"She did," Brendan said. "And she has evidence."

"What evidence?" Josie asked. He had to be bluffing or at least exaggerating the evidentiary value of what he'd found. She'd gone through those folders so many times but hadn't figured out what he'd discerned so quickly.

Margaret snorted. "Evidence. It doesn't matter. It's never going to get to court. I will never be arrested."

That was Josie's concern, too. And then Brendan's name would never be cleared.

"I already brought the evidence to the district attorney," Brendan said, answering one of Josie's questions.

Now she knew where he'd been. He had gone through the right channels for justice.

"The arrest warrant should have been issued by now," Brendan continued. But he was looking at her henchman instead of Margaret, as if warning him. Or trying to use his bluff to scare him off. "Do you want to go to jail with her?"

"I had nothing to do with her killing your dad," the man said. "I didn't even work for her then."

"But you're working for her now," Brendan said. "You've assaulted a woman and threatened the life of a child. I think those charges will put you away for a while, too, especially if you're already on parole for other crimes."

The man's face flushed with color. He shook his head, but not in denial of his criminal record. Instead he pulled the gun away from Josie and murmured, "I'm sorry."

"Don't let him get to you," Margaret said. "He's bluffing. He's just bluffing."

The man shook his head again, obviously unwilling to risk it. It wasn't as if they were playing poker for money. They were playing for prison.

"Where are you going?" Margaret screamed after him as he headed for the door. "How dare you desert me!"

The man was lucky that she was having a standoff with Brendan or she probably would have fired a bullet into his back. She was that furious.

"You should just give it up," Josie told her. "You have no help now."

Margaret glared. "Neither does he."

"He has me," Josie said.

"Not for long," Margaret said. "He's going to lose you just like you're going to lose that brat of yours."

"You just shut the hell up," Josie warned the woman, her temper fraying from the threats and insults directed at CJ. "Don't ever talk about my son."

Margaret chuckled, so Josie struck her. She'd hoped to knock the gun from the petite woman's hand. But the older lady was surprisingly strong. She held on to her gun and swung it toward Josie, pressing it into her heart—which was exactly what her insults and threats had been hitting.

"You get involved with a killer, sooner or later you're going to wind up dead," the woman said. "Too bad for you it's going to be sooner."

Wasn't it already later—since Margaret had first tried to kill her four years ago? But Josie kept that question to herself.

"You're the killer," Brendan corrected Margaret. So she would have no compunction pulling the trigger and killing Josie. It was what she'd intended to do from the moment she'd forced her inside the house. That was why she'd confessed to her—because she planned to make sure Josie could never testify against her.

"If you had really turned over proof to the district attorney, the police would be here already," Margaret said. "You have nothing."

"You confessed to Josie."

"Just now," she said. "And she'll never live to testify against me."

"No," he said, "you confessed to her four years ago."

Margaret laughed. "She doesn't even know what evidence you had. I think she damn well would have known had I confessed to her."

"You weren't confessing," Brendan admitted. "You were trying to convince her of my guilt. You told her that it must have been someone he trusted since my father had never pulled his gun."

Josie gasped. "And all the other reports—except for the official police report—claimed he'd been killed with his own gun."

Since Dennis O'Hannigan was legendary for turning a person's weapon on them, it had been the height of irony that he'd had his own gun turned on him.

Brendan shook his head. "But all his guns were in their holsters." He'd learned from his father to have more than one backup weapon. "Only the killer would know that he hadn't pulled any of them, that he'd trusted his killer."

Margaret snorted. "Trusted? Hell, no. Underestimated is what he'd done. He thought I was too weak and helpless to be a threat."

"And he would have considered me a threat," Brendan said, because his father had known what his son had become. What he really was.

So why had he left him the business?

"You underestimated me, too," she accused Brendan. "You never considered me a threat, either."

He hadn't realized just how dangerous she was—until she'd turned her gun on the woman he loved. "It's over, Margaret."

"On that flimsy evidence?" she asked, nearly as incredulous as the district attorney had been.

"No, on the confession that the FBI has recorded."

She glanced at Josie as if checking her for a wire.

"When your security system was hacked, the house was bugged. Every intercom in the place turned on like a mike."

She glanced around at the intercom by the door and another on the desk behind her.

"You're under arrest for the murder of Dennis O'Hannigan," he said, "and the attempted murders of Josie Jessup and—"

The woman raised her eyebrows and scoffed. "You're arresting me? On what authority?"

"FBI," he said. "I'm an FBI agent."

Josie's eyes widened with surprise. He'd hoped that she might have figured it out, that she would have realized he was not a bad man.

"You are not," Margaret said. "You're bluffing again, treating me like a fool just like your father did."

With his free hand he pulled out his credentials, which he hadn't been able to carry for the past four years, and flashed his shield at her. "No. Game over."

She stubbornly shook her head and threatened, "I am going to pull the trigger."

"Then so will I," he replied. And he was bluffing now.

"You won't risk her life." Margaret knowingly called

him on his lie. "I saw how you were when she disappeared four years ago. You were as devastated as you were when your mother disappeared."

He couldn't deny the truth—not anymore.

"So you're going to step back and let me leave with her," Margaret said.

"And what do you think you're going to do?" Brendan asked. "Talk her into taking you to our son?"

Margaret's gaze darted between him and Josie. That had been her plan—all part of her deranged plan.

"She'll never do that," Brendan said. "You won't be able to kill all the O'Hannigans. And even if you thought you did, you still wouldn't be the last one." He chuckled now at how incredibly flawed the woman's plan was. "You're actually not even a real O'Hannigan."

Anger tightened her lips into a thin line. "I married your father."

"But it wasn't legal," he informed her.

She glared at him. "I have the license to prove it, since you're all about evidence."

"It wasn't legal because he was still married," he explained.

"What?" she gasped.

"My mother isn't dead."

"Yes, she is," Margaret frantically insisted. "Your father killed her. Everyone knows that."

"He'd beaten her...." Which Brendan had witnessed; he'd been only eleven years old and helpless to protect her. "He sent her to the hospital, but she didn't die. She went into witness protection."

But still she wouldn't testify against him. Not because she had still loved the man but because she'd loved Brendan. And to protect him, she had struck a bargain with the devil.

Maybe he would have to do the same to protect Josie.

"You're lying," Margaret said. She was distracted now, more focused on him than Josie.

He shook his head, keeping her attention on him while he tried to ignore Special Agent Martinez speaking through his earpiece. Brendan was calling the shots now. And he wouldn't do that until Josie was out of the line of fire.

"Where do you think I ran away to when I was fifteen?" he asked. Thank God he hadn't wound up living on the streets, which he'd been desperate enough to do. He'd found a place to go. A home.

"I didn't think you really ran away," Margaret said. "I know you tried, that you stole one of your father's cars. But that car was returned that same night— without you. And you were never seen again."

As he relived that night, his heart flipped with the fear he'd felt when his father's men had driven him off the road and into the ditch. At fifteen he hadn't had enough experience behind the wheel to be able to outmaneuver them. And when they'd jerked him from behind the wheel and left him alone with his father, he'd thought he was dead, that he'd be going to see his mother in heaven.

His father had sent him to her with a bus ticket and a slip of paper with an address on it. His mother had been relocated to New York, where she had built a life fostering runaway kids. And somehow, either using money or threats, Dennis had found out exactly what had happened to his wife and where she was. Brendan had used that bus ticket to reunite with her and become one of those kids. And in exchange for getting her son back, his mother had agreed to never testify against Dennis O'Hannigan.

"My mom will actually be here soon," he said with a glance at Josie. "But the other agents will be here before her."

That was the cue, sent through his headset, to make all hell break loose.

Chapter Seventeen

Josie was reeling from all the answers she'd just received to questions she hadn't even known to ask. Was it true? Was any of it true?

Brendan had flashed the badge, but she hadn't had a chance to read it. Was it *his* name on it? Was he really an FBI agent? And what about his mother being alive all these years in witness protection?

It all seemed so unrealistic that it almost had to be real. And it explained so much.

She heard the footsteps then. And so did Margaret. Before the woman could react and pull the trigger, Josie shoved her back and then dropped to the floor as shots rang out.

The house exploded. There was no bomb, but the effects were the same. Glass shattered. Footsteps pounded. Voices shouted. And shots were fired.

She wasn't sure she would feel if any bullets struck her. She was numb with shock. She'd thought she had fooled and deceived Brendan four years ago. But she had been the fool. In her search for what she'd thought was the truth, she had fallen for the lies. This woman's lies. The other news reports about him.

He could have set her straight, but he had chosen instead to keep his secrets. And to let her go…

A hand clutched her hair, pulling her head up as a barrel pressed again to her temple. How many times could a gun be held to her head before it was fired? Either on purpose or accidentally?

Josie worried that her luck was about to run out.

"Let her go!" Brendan shouted the order. And cocked his gun.

Another shot rang out, along with a soft click, and Josie flinched, waiting for the pain to explode in her head. But then Margaret dropped to the floor beside her, blood spurting from her shoulder. Her eyes wide open with shock, she stared into Josie's face. Then she began to curse, calling Josie every vulgar name as agents jerked her to her feet.

Then there were hands on Josie's arms, hands that shook a little as they helped her up. Her legs wobbled and she pitched slightly forward, falling into a broad chest. Strong arms closed around her, holding her steady.

"Are you all right?" Brendan asked, his deep voice gruff with emotion.

She wasn't sure. "How—how did she not shoot me… when she got shot?"

"She'd already fired all her bullets," he replied.

She realized the soft click she'd heard had been from the empty cartridge. "Did you know?"

"I counted."

How? In the chaos of the raid, how had he kept track of it all? But then she remembered that he was a professional. She was the amateur, the one who hadn't belonged in his world four years ago and certainly didn't belong there now.

She belonged with her son. She should have never left him.

Exhausted, she laid her head on his chest. His heart beat as frantically as hers, both feeling the aftereffects of adrenaline and fear. At least Josie had been afraid.

She wasn't sure how Brendan felt about anything. She hadn't even known who he really was.

PARAMEDICS HAD PUT her in the back of an ambulance, but she had refused to lie down on the stretcher. She sat up on it, her legs dangling over the side. She wasn't a small woman, yet there was something childlike about her now, Brendan thought. She looked…lost.

"Is she okay?" he asked the paramedic who'd stepped out of the ambulance to talk quietly to him.

"Except for some bruises, she's physically all right," the paramedic assured him. "But she does appear to be in shock."

Was that because she'd been held and threatened by a crazy woman? Or because she had finally learned the truth about him?

"It looks like you were hit," the paramedic re-marked, reaching up toward Brendan's head. He hadn't been hit, but not for lack of trying on his stepmother's part. As lousy a shot as she was, she must have been very close to his father to have killed him.

Too close for his father to have seen how dangerous the woman really was. His father had been so smart and careful when it came to business. Why had he'd been so sloppy and careless when it had come to pleasure?

Four years ago, when Brendan had found out his lover was really a reporter after a story, he'd thought he had been careless, too. And his carelessness had nearly gotten Josie killed.

"I'm fine," he told the paramedic. "That's not even recent." Two nights ago seemed like a lifetime ago. But then it had been a different life, one that Brendan didn't need to live anymore. He'd found the justice for which he'd started searching four years ago.

As he watched an agent load a bandaged and handcuffed Margaret into the back of a federal car, he knew he had justice. But he held up a hand to halt the car. Her wounded shoulder had already been treated, so she'd been medically cleared to be booked. But he didn't want them booking her yet, not before he knew all the charges against her.

"It's not scabbed over yet," the young woman persisted, as she continued to inspect the scratch on Brendan's head.

"I'm fine. But maybe you should double check the suspect," he suggested. After the paramedic left, he turned back toward the ambulance and found Josie staring at him.

She had lost that stunned look of shock. Her brow was furrowed, her eyes dark, and she looked mad. She had every right to be angry—furious, even. "I'm sorry," he said.

"Are you sorry that you saved my life?" she asked. "Or are you sorry that you lied to me?"

"I never lied."

She nodded her head sharply in agreement. "You didn't have to. You just let me make all my wrong assumptions and you never bothered to correct me. Is that why you're sorry?"

"I'm sorry," he said, "because I never should have gotten involved with you—not when I had just started the most dangerous assignment of my career." But he'd been sloppy and careless. He'd let his attraction to her overcome his common sense.

Special Agent Martinez had urged him to go for it, that having a girlfriend gave Brendan a better cover and made him look more like his dad. That it might have roused suspicions if he'd turned down such a beautiful woman. But Brendan couldn't blame Martinez. It hadn't been an order, more so a suggestion. Brendan hadn't had to listen to him.

It was all his fault—everything Josie had been through, everything she'd lost. She hadn't died, but she'd still lost her home, her family, her career. If only he'd stayed away from her…

If only he'd resisted his attraction to her…

But he'd never felt anything as powerful.

"You thought I was going to blow your cover," she said. "That's why you didn't tell me what was going on. You didn't trust that I wouldn't go public with the story."

"I know you, Josie. You can't stop being a reporter," he reminded her. "Even after they relocated you, you were ferreting out stories."

"But if you had asked me not to print anything, I would have held off," she said. "I wouldn't have put your life in danger."

No. He was the one who'd put her life in danger. And he understood that she would probably never be able to forgive him, especially if her father didn't make it.

"But you didn't trust me," she said.

"You didn't trust me, either," he said, "or you wouldn't have raced here to make sure I didn't kill Margaret for vigilante justice. You still suspected that I might be a killer."

"I didn't know who you really are," she said.

She hadn't known what he really did for a living, but she should have known what kind of person he was. Since she hadn't, there was no way that she could love him.

"How did you figure out where I had gone?" he asked. "You had all that information for years, but you never put it together. And then I took everything to present to the district attorney. So how did you realize it was Margaret?"

"CJ told me."

He laughed at her ridiculous claim. "CJ? How did he figure it out?"

"*You* told him," she said, "when you told him that you were going to get rid of the bad person so he'd be safe."

He hadn't even known if the little boy was truly awake when he'd told him goodbye. It was wanting to make sure that goodbye wasn't permanent that had had Brendan going through the proper channels for the arrest warrant.

"You said bad *person*," she said, "not bad man, like we'd been telling him the shooters and the bomber was. Since Margaret was the only female I'd talked to about your father's murder, it had to be her."

He glanced to that car where his stepmother sat and waited for him. He needed to question her. But he dreaded leaving Josie after he had nearly lost her. He couldn't even blink without horrible images replaying in his mind—the burly man slapping her so hard her neck snapped and then the gun pressed to her temple…

Josie shivered as she followed his gaze. "I need to get home to CJ. I need to make sure he's safe."

"You don't need to go home," he said. "He should be here very soon."

Her brow furrowed. "How? Is Charlotte bringing him?"

"Charlotte couldn't come." He wondered if the former U.S. marshal had had her baby yet. "So I sent someone else to get him from Mrs. Mallory's."

She clutched his arm with a shaking hand. "You shouldn't have trusted anyone else, not with our son.

"I sent the only person I trust," he said.

She shivered again as if his words had chilled her. He didn't mean to hurt her feelings, but he hadn't been able to trust her—any more than she had been able to trust him.

The arrival of another vehicle, a minivan, drew their attention to the driveway. He smiled as an older woman jumped out of the driver's seat and pulled open the sliding door to the back. A redheaded little boy raised his arms and encircled the woman's neck as she lifted him from his booster seat.

"Looks like CJ likes his grandma," he murmured.

Josie gasped. "That's your mother? She really is alive?"

The dark, curly-haired woman was small, like Margaret, but she had so much energy and vibrancy. She would never be mistaken for fragile. She was the strongest woman he had ever known...until he'd witnessed Josie's fearlessness over and over again. She would have taken a bullet in the brain before she would have ever led Margaret to their son.

Almost too choked with emotion over seeing his mom and son together, Brendan only nodded. Then he cleared his throat and added, "My dangerous assignment is over now." And given what he now knew he had to lose, he didn't intend to ever go undercover again. "So I'd like to have a relationship with my son."

"Of course," she immediately agreed. "I'm glad he's met your mother. She sounds like an amazing woman. She gave up so much for you."

Just as Josie would have for their son. For him, Brendan's mother had given up justice for all the pain his father had put her through.

He nodded. "She is."

Josie smiled as the little boy giggled in his grandmother's arms as she tickled him. "I would like CJ to meet my father now—if you think it's safe."

"It's all over now," Brendan assured her. "Margaret knows that. Anyone who worked for her knows that now." The burly guard was sitting in the back of another car. Agents had apprehended him as he'd hightailed it out of the house. "It will be safe."

She bit her bottom lip and sighed. "For us. I'm not sure how safe it'll be for my father though. I don't want to risk giving him another heart attack. It's bad enough that he was attacked to draw me out of hiding."

And that was probably his fault, too—Margaret's wanting to make sure no other O'Hannigan heirs stood in the way of her greed. He needed to interview the crazy woman and find out who she'd been working with—who she'd bought.

"I'm sorry," he said again. He couldn't apologize enough for the danger in which he'd put Josie and their son.

BRENDAN WANTED A relationship with his son but not her. Would he never trust her? Would he never forgive her for deceiving him?

He had deceived her, too. Of course he'd had his reasons. And his orders. He couldn't tell her the truth and risk her blowing his cover.

Now she understood why he'd been so angry with her when he'd realized she had initially sought him out for an exposé. It hadn't been just a matter of pride. It had been a matter of life and death.

After all the times she'd been shot at and nearly blown up, she understood how dangerous his life was. That was why he'd kept apologizing to her.

He'd said he was sorry, but he'd never said what she'd wanted to hear. That he loved her.

She sighed.

"Everything all right, miss?" the driver asked.

She glanced into the back of the government Suburban where CJ's booster seat had been buckled. Her son was safe and happy. Of course he hadn't wanted to leave his daddy or his grandma, but he'd agreed when she'd explained he was going to meet his grandpa.

"Yes, I just hope that my dad is better." That he would be strong enough to handle the surprise of seeing her alive and well.

The older man nodded. She hadn't noticed him during all the turmoil earlier in Margaret's house. He didn't have a scratch on his bald head or a wrinkle in his dark suit. Maybe he hadn't been part of the rescue. Maybe he'd been in the van that they'd passed as they'd left the estate.

"Thank you for driving me to the hospital, Agent…"

"Marshal," he replied. "I'm a U.S. marshal."

"Did Charlotte send you?" she asked. Brendan had told her why her friend had been unable to come to her aid herself; she was having a baby. She hadn't even known Charlotte was pregnant. It had to be Aaron Timmer's baby. Josie had realized her friend was falling for her former bodyguard shortly after he'd been hired to work palace security, too. Had they married? She'd been so preoccupied with her own life lately that she hadn't gotten the specifics of what Charlotte and Princess Gabriella had endured.

"Charlotte?" the man repeated the name.

"Charlotte Green," Josie explained. "She was the marshal who relocated me in the program."

The man nodded. "Yes, she didn't tell anyone else where she'd placed you. Not even her partner."

Josie shuddered as she thought of the man who would have killed to learn her whereabouts. He must have been working for Margaret O'Hannigan. But then why had the woman thought she was dead?

"It's a shame that Trigger was killed."

"In self-defense." Josie defended her former bodyguard. Whit was the one who'd found the bomb in the safe house and called the marshals. Everything had moved so quickly after that—Josie had moved so quickly.

"He was a friend."

Josie shivered now and glanced back at CJ to make sure he was all right. "Trigger was a friend of yours?"

"Yes, a close friend. We used to work together," he said. "But then things happened in my life. I took a leave from work and lost Trigger as my partner with the Marshals. We also lost touch for a while…until recently. Then we reconnected."

"You had talked to him recently?" she asked.

"Right before he died…"

"Do you know who he was working for?" Josie asked. It might help the district attorney's case against Margaret to have a witness who could corroborate that she'd hired the hit on her.

"He wasn't working for anyone," the man replied. "He was doing a favor for a friend."

God, no...

She realized that this man was the friend for whom Trigger had been doing the favor. This man was the one who'd wanted her location, and from the nerves tightening her stomach into knots, she suspected he had not wanted her found in order to wish her well. She glanced down at her bag lying on the floor at her feet. Could she reach inside without his noticing? She didn't have the gun anymore. It had been left at the crime scene back at Margaret O'Hannigan's house. But if she could get to her phone...

She couldn't call Charlotte, but she could call Brendan. He would come; he would save her and their son as he had so many times over the past few days.

She should have trusted him four years ago. If she had showed him the information she'd compiled, they would have figured out together that it was Margaret who had killed his father. But apprehending Margaret earlier wouldn't have kept Josie safe.

"You were the friend?" she asked, as she leaned down and reached for her purse.

"If you're looking for this," he remarked as he lifted a cell phone from under his thigh, "don't bother." The driver's window lowered, and he tossed out the phone. "That way Charlotte Green's little GPS device won't be able to track you down."

He must have taken the phone from her purse while she'd been buckling CJ into his seat in the back. She was so tired that she hadn't even been aware of what the man was doing. She had barely been aware of him.

"Who are you?" she asked, her heart beating fast with panic and dread.

"You don't recognize me?"

She was afraid to look directly at him. A hostage

was never supposed to look at her kidnapper. If she couldn't identify him, he might let her live.

But as her blood chilled, she realized this wasn't a kidnapper. Unlike Margaret O'Hannigan, this person wasn't interested in money. He had an entirely different agenda.

"I—I don't know," she replied, but she was staring down at her purse, wondering what might have been left inside that she could use as a weapon. "I've been away for so many years."

"You're the one who looks different," he said. "But I know the doctor Charlotte Green sends witnesses to, so I got him to show me your files. I knew what you'd look like. I recognized you in the parking garage."

"That—that was you?" she asked.

He nodded his head. "And the other so-called orderly was at O'Hannigan's place, setting up the backup plan."

She glanced again at CJ and whispered, "The bomb?"

"But you were just so quick," he murmured regretfully. "Too quick."

"And Brendan's apartment?"

"I have a friend with the Bureau, one who knew that your little mob friend is really an agent, so he knew where his safe house is."

The guy had gotten to another marshal and an agent. Which agent? Were Brendan and his mother safe?

"Is—is this agent going to hurt Brendan?"

He chuckled. "He thinks O'Hannigan walks on water. He didn't realize why I was asking about the guy."

"He'll put it together now," she warned him. "Since the bomb and the shooting."

The man shook his head. "No. No one would ever consider me capable of what I've done and what I'm about to do."

"Because you're a U.S. marshal?"

"Because I'm a good marshal," he said, "and I've always been a good man."

Then maybe he would change his mind. Maybe he wouldn't shoot her and her son.…

"But you and your father changed all that," he said. "That's why you have to pay. You and your father took everything from me, everything that mattered. So now I'm going to do that to your father. I'm going to take away what matters most to him. Again."

So even four years ago, this man had been the one—the one who'd cut her brakes and set up the bomb. All of it had been because of him.

"Mr. Peterson," she murmured as recognition dawned. How had she not remembered that Donny Peterson's father was a U.S. marshal? Her former college classmate had brought it up enough, using it as a threat against whoever challenged him. She hadn't heeded that threat, though; she'd continued to pursue the story that had led to Donny's destruction. So all of it had been because of *her*.

Neither of the bombs or the shootings at the hospital and the apartment complex had had anything to do with Brendan's job, his family or his relationship with her.

It was all her fault and she was about to pay for that with her life. But Brendan, who'd had nothing to do with it, would pay, too—when he lost his son.

"Now you know who I am."

If only she'd realized it earlier…

If only she and CJ hadn't gotten inside the SUV with him.

"I understand why you're upset," she assured him, hoping to reason with him. "But you should be upset with me. Not with my son. Not with my father."

"You fed him the information, but he wrote the damn story." He snorted derisively. "Jess Ley."

"I'm Jess Ley," she corrected him. "I wrote the story."

He sucked in a breath as if she'd struck him. He hadn't known. "But if your father hadn't printed it and broadcast it everywhere…"

His son might still be alive.

"That was my fault," she said.

She alone had caused this man's pain—as she was about to cause Brendan's. Because this man must have originally planned to take her from her father in his quest for an eye for an eye. Now he would also take her son from her.

Chapter Eighteen

"I think you should have gone with them to the hospital," his mother chastised Brendan.

While other agents slapped him on the back to express their approval, his mother leaned against her minivan with her arms crossed. Her brown eyes, which were usually so warm and crinkled at the corners with a smile, were dark and narrowed with disapproval.

"I have to talk to Margaret," he said.

"Why?" she asked with a glance at the car in which her husband's killer sat. "She confessed, right?"

"To killing my father," Brendan said.

"Isn't that all you need?" she asked. "It's not like there's any mystery as to why."

He shook his head. "No, she explained that, too. Dad was going to divorce her and leave her with nothing. She wanted it all. That must be why she wanted to hurt Josie and my son, why she wanted to kill them, too—to make sure there were no more O'Hannigans."

"Your father's damn codicil," she remarked.

He grinned as his mother and stepmother glared at each other through the back window of the police car. "She didn't know about you."

His mother shrugged. "Doesn't matter. I'm not an O'Hannigan anymore."

No. She'd dropped her married name when the marshals had moved her. To the runaways she'd fostered, she'd been just Roma. Perhaps they'd all known the Jones surname was an alias.

"She thought you were dead," Brendan remarked as he opened the back door to the police car.

"What the hell is it with you people?" Margaret asked. "Is anyone really dead?" She turned her glare on Brendan. "First you come back from the dead and show up to claim what was mine. And then your nosy girlfriend comes back from the dead with a kid. And now her..." She curled her thin lips in disgust.

He'd been so scared that Josie had been alone with a suspected killer that he hadn't been paying much attention to the conversation coming through the mike. But now he remembered Margaret's surprise that Josie wasn't dead. He'd thought it was because she'd incorrectly assumed Josie had been killed with him from the bomb set at his house, but he realized now that she'd never admitted to planting it.

But why? When she had confessed to murder, why would she bother denying attempted murder?

"You didn't know Josie was alive?" he asked.

She shrugged. "I didn't care whether she was or not until she showed up here with pictures of your damn kid in her purse and all those damn questions of hers. How could you have not realized she was a reporter?"

Especially given who her father was. Brendan had been a fool to not realize it. But then he hadn't been thinking clearly. He never did around her.

He had just let Josie walk off with their son before

he'd confirmed that she was safe. Hell, he'd told her she was—that Margaret wouldn't be a threat anymore. But had Margaret ever been the threat to Josie?

"You didn't know Josie was in witness relocation?"

"I didn't know that anybody was in witness relocation," the woman replied. A calculating look came over her face. "But perhaps I should talk to the marshals, let them know what I know about your father's business and his associates."

Despite foreboding clutching his stomach muscles into tight knots, he managed a short chuckle. "I gave them everything there was to know." Along with the men who'd disappeared—either into prisons or the program.

"You have nothing to offer anyone anymore, Margaret," he said as he slammed the door. Then he pounded on the roof, giving the go-ahead for the driver to pull away and take her to jail. He couldn't hear her as the car drove off, but he could read her lips and realized she was cursing him.

But he was already cursing himself. "Where did Josie go?" he asked his mother.

"To see her father," she said, as if he were being stupid again. "You and I should have gone along. I could have talked to her father and prepared him for seeing his daughter again after he spent the past four years believing she was dead."

"Yeah, because you prepared *me* so well," he said. He nearly hadn't gone to the address his father had given him. But after he'd gotten off the bus, he'd been scared and hungry and cold. So he'd gone to the house and knocked on the door. And when she'd opened it, he'd passed out. Later he'd blamed the hunger and the cold, but it was probably because he'd thought he'd seen a ghost.

It had taken him years to live down the razzing from Roma's other runaways.

"You're right," he said. "I should have gone with her."

"Do you know which hospital?"

He nodded. He knew the hospital well. He just didn't know how she'd gotten there. "What vehicle did she take?"

Roma shook her head. "She got a ride in a black SUV."

"With whom?"

"A marshal, I think. The guy had his badge on a chain around his neck." That was how the men who'd taken her into the program had worn theirs, or so she'd told him when she'd explained how she had disappeared. "He offered to drive her and CJ to see her father."

How had the man known that her father was in the hospital? And why had a marshal walked into the middle of an FBI investigation? The two agencies worked together, but usually not willingly and not without withholding more information than they shared.

Brendan had become an FBI agent instead of a marshal because he'd resented the marshals for not letting his mother take him along—for making him mourn her for years, as he'd mourned Josie.

He had a bad feeling that he might be mourning her again. And CJ, too, if he didn't find her. Charlotte wouldn't have sent another marshal; she had trusted Brendan to keep Josie and their son safe.

And he had a horrible feeling, as his heart ached with the force of its frantic pounding, that he had failed.

"WHY—WHY DID you bring us here?" Josie asked as she rode up in the hospital elevator with her son and a madman.

Before Donald Peterson could reply, CJ answered, "We came to see Grampa." He'd even pushed the button to the sixth floor. "We shoulda brought Gramma."

No. Brendan was already going to lose one person he loved—if Josie didn't think of something to at least save their son. She didn't want him to lose his mother, too.

She looked up at their captor. "We should have left him with his grandmother," she said. "And his father. He isn't part of this."

"He's your son," Peterson said. "Your father's grandson. He's very much a part of this."

She shook her head. "He's a three-year-old child. He has nothing to do with any of this."

The elevator lurched to a halt on the sixth floor, nearly making her stomach lurch, too, with nerves and fear. With a gun shoved in the middle of her back, the U.S. marshal pushed her out the open doors. She held tight to CJ's hand.

He kept digging the gun deeper, pushing her down the hall toward her father's room. A man waited outside. He was dressed like an orderly, as he'd been dressed the night he'd held Brendan back from getting on the elevator with her and CJ. She'd been grateful for his intervention then.

He wasn't going to intervene tonight—just as his partners in crime had refused to be swayed from the U.S. marshal's nefarious plan. But still she had to try. "Please," she said, "you don't want to be part of this."

"He's already part of it," Peterson replied. "Even

before he set the bomb, he was already wanted for other crimes."

She understood now. "You tracked them down on their outstanding warrants but you worked out a deal for not bringing them in."

Peterson chuckled. "You can't stop asking questions, can't stop trying to ferret out all the information you can."

She shuddered, remembering that Brendan had accused her of the same thing. No wonder he hadn't been able to trust her.

"But you and your father won't be able to broadcast this story," he said.

"You're not going to get away," she warned him.

"I know. But it's better this way—better to see his face and yours than have someone else take the pleasure for me." He pushed the barrel deeper into her back and ordered, "Open the door."

"I—I think someone should warn him first," she said. "Let him know that I'm alive so that he doesn't have another heart attack."

"It was unfortunate that he had the first one," Peterson agreed. "He was only supposed to be hurt, not killed." He glanced at the orderly as he said that, as if the man had not followed orders. "But the doctors have put him on medication to regulate his heart. He's probably stronger now than he was when he thought you died four years ago. That didn't kill him."

His mouth tightened. "It would be easier to die," he said, "than to lose a child and have to live."

He wasn't worried about getting away anymore, because he had obviously decided to end his life, too.

"I'm sorry," she murmured.

"Not yet," he replied, "but you will be." He pushed her through the door to her father's room.

"Stop shoving my mommy!" CJ yelled at him. "You're a bad man!"

"What—what's going on?" asked the gray-haired man in the room. He was sitting up as if he'd been about to get out of bed. He was bruised, but he wasn't broken. "Who are you all? Are you in the right room?"

"Yes," CJ replied. "This is my grampa's room number. Are you my grampa?"

Stanley Jessup looked at his grandson through narrowed eyes. Then he lifted his gaze and looked at Josie. At first he didn't recognize her; his brow furrowed as if he tried to place her, though.

"You don't know your own daughter?" the U.S. marshal berated him. "I would know my son anywhere. No matter what he may have done to his face, I would recognize his soul. That's how I knew he couldn't have done the things that article and those news reports said." He raised the gun and pointed it at Josie's head. "The things—the lies—your friend told you, claiming that my Donny had tried to hurt her."

"Donald Peterson," her father murmured. He recognized her attempted killer but not his own daughter.

"Your son told me, too," Josie said. "He had once been my friend, too."

"Until you betrayed him."

"Until he tried to rape my roommate," she said. If not for her coming to her father with the article, he might have gotten away with it—just as he'd gotten away with his drug use—but the athletic director hadn't wanted to lose their star player from the football team. So they'd tried paying off the girl. When she'd refused money, they'd expelled her and labeled her crazy.

So just as she had done with Margaret O'Hannigan today, Josie had gotten Donny Peterson to confess.

"Josie…" Her father whispered her name, as if unable to believe it. Then he looked down at the little boy, who stared up at him in puzzlement.

Poor CJ had been through so much the past few days. He'd met so many people and had been in so much danger, he had to be thoroughly confused and exhausted. He whispered, too, to his grandfather, "He's a bad man, Grampa."

"Your mama and grandpa are the bad ones," Donald Peterson insisted. "My Donny was a star, and they couldn't handle it. They had to bring him down, had to destroy him."

After the confession and the subsequent charges, Donny Peterson had killed himself, shortly before the trial was to begin, shortly before Josie's brakes were cut. Why hadn't she considered that those attempts might have been because of Donny? Why had she automatically thought the worst of Brendan? Maybe because she'd already been feeling guilty and hadn't wanted to admit to how much to blame she'd been.

"And that is why I'm going to destroy them," Donald continued.

"You're a bad man," CJ said again, and he kicked the man in the shin.

Josie tried to grab her son before the man could strike back. But he was already swinging and his hand struck Josie's cheek, sending her stumbling back onto her father's bed. Stanley Jessup caught her shoulders and then pulled her and his grandson close, as if his arms alone could protect them.

CJ wriggled in their grasp as he tried to break free to fight some more. "My daddy told me to p'tect you," he reminded Josie. "I have to p'tect my mommy until my daddy gets here."

Donald Peterson shook his head. "Your daddy's not coming, son."

"My daddy's a hero," CJ said. "He'll be here. He always saves us."

"It is a daddy's job to protect his kids," Donald agreed, his voice cracking with emotion. "But your daddy's busy arresting some bad people."

"You're bad."

"And he's too far away to get here to help you."

Tears began to streak down CJ's face, and his shoulders shook as fear overcame him. He'd been so brave for her—so brave for his father. But now he was scared.

And Josie could offer him no words of comfort. As Donald Peterson had stated, there was no way that Brendan could reach them in time to save them.

They had to figure out a way to save themselves. Her father shifted on his bed and pressed something cold and metallic against Josie's hip. A gun. Had he had it under his pillow?

After the assault, she couldn't blame him for wanting to be prepared if his attacker tried again. But Donald's gun barrel was trained on CJ. And she knew—to make her father and her feel the loss he felt—he would shoot her son first. Could she grab the gun, aim and fire before he killed her little boy?

THE CAMERAS HAD still been running inside the van, and they'd caught the plate on the black SUV that had driven off with Brendan's son and the woman he loved. The vehicle had a GPS that had led them right to its location in the parking garage of the hospital.

When they'd arrived, Brendan hadn't gone down to

check it out. He already knew where they were. So he ducked under the whirling FBI helicopter blades and ran across the roof where just a few nights ago he'd nearly been shot. Once he was inside the elevator, he pushed the button for the sixth floor.

It seemed to take forever to get where he needed to be.

His mom was right. He should have taken Josie here. He never should have let her and CJ out of his sight. And if he wasn't already too late, he never would.

Finally the elevator stopped and the doors slowly opened. He had barely stepped from the car when a shot or two rang out. He fired back. And his aim was better.

The pseudo-orderly dropped to the floor, clutching his bleeding arm. His gun dropped, too. Brendan kicked it aside as he hurried past the man. The orderly wasn't the one who'd driven off with his family. He wasn't the one with the grudge against Josie.

That man was already inside and he had nothing to lose. Running the plate had tied it to the marshal to whom the vehicle had been assigned, and a simple Google search on the helicopter ride had revealed the rest of Donald Peterson's tragic story. There was no point in calling out, no point in trying to negotiate with him. The only thing he wanted was Josie dead— as dead as his son.

So Brendan kicked open the door, sending it flying back against the wall. He had his gun raised, ready to fire, but his finger froze on the trigger.

The man holding a gun was not the marshal but the patient. The marshal lay on the floor, blood pooling beneath his shoulder. His eyes were closed, tears trickling from their corners. But his pain wasn't physical.

It was a pain Brendan had nearly felt himself. Of loss and helplessness…

"See, I knew my daddy would make it," CJ said, his voice high with excitement and a trace of hysteria. "I knew he would save us."

Brendan glanced down at the floor again, checking for the man's weapon. But Josie held it. He looked back at his son. "Doesn't look like you needed saving at all. Your mommy and grandpa had it all under control."

Stanley Jessup shook his head. "If you hadn't distracted him with the shooting outside the door, I never would have been able to…" He shuddered. While the man was a damn good marksman, he wasn't comfortable with having shot a person.

"Are you okay, Daddy?" Josie asked.

He grabbed her, pulling her into his arms. "I am now. A couple of nights ago I heard a scream and then a female voice, and I recognized it. But I didn't dare hope. I thought it was the painkillers. I couldn't let myself believe. Couldn't let myself hope… You're alive…"

"I'm so sorry!" she exclaimed, her body shaking with sobs. "I'm so sorry."

It was a poignant moment, but one that was short-lived as police officers and hospital security burst into the room. It was nearly an hour later before the men had been arrested and the explanations made.

Finally Stanley Jessup could have a moment alone with his daughter and grandson, so Brendan stepped outside and pulled the door closed behind him. He walked over to his mother, who had insisted on coming along in the helicopter with him and the other agents.

"I'm going to get some coffee and food," Roma said. "I'm sure my grandson is hungry. He's had a long day." She rose on tiptoe and pressed a kiss to Brendan's cheek. "So has my son."

"It's not over yet," he said.

Her brow furrowed slightly. "Isn't it all over? All the bad people arrested?"

"There's still something I need to do," Brendan said. For him it wasn't all over. It was just beginning.

She nodded as if she understood. She probably did; his mother had always known what was in his heart.

Josie didn't, but he intended to tell her.

After patting his cheek with her palm, his mother headed down the hall and disappeared into the elevator, leaving him alone. He had spent so much of his life alone—those years before he'd joined his mother in witness protection. Then all the years he'd gone undercover—deep undercover—for the Bureau. He'd been young when he'd started working for the FBI, since his last name had given him an easy entrance to any criminal organization the Bureau had wanted to investigate. And take down.

He had taken down several of the most violent gangs and dangerous alliances. But none of them had realized he was the one responsible.

If the truth about him came out now, his family could be in danger of retaliation—revenge like that the marshal had wanted against the Jessups because of the loss of his son.

Pain clutched Brendan's heart as he thought of how close he had come to losing his son. CJ had told him how he'd tried to "p'tect" his mommy as he'd promised. The brave little three-year-old had kicked the man with the gun.

He shuddered at what could have happened had Josie

obviously not taken the blow meant for their boy. She'd had a fresh mark on her face.

As she stepped out of her father's room and joined him in the hall, he studied her face. The red mark was already darkening. He found himself reaching up and touching her cheek as he murmured, "I should have kicked him, too."

She flinched. "I used to worry that CJ was too timid," she said, "but now I worry that he might be too brave."

"Are you surprised?" he asked. "You've always been fearless."

"Careless," she corrected him. "I didn't care about the consequences. I didn't realize what could happen to me."

He'd thought that was because she'd been spoiled, that she'd been her father's princess and believed he would never let anything happen to her. Now Brendan realized that she'd cared more about others than herself.

"You're the brave one," she said. "You've put your-self in danger to protect others. To protect me. Thank you."

He shook his head. He didn't want her gratitude. He wanted her love.

"I thought you might have left with the others," she said, glancing around the empty hall. "With your mom…"

"She's still here," he said. "She's getting food and coming back up." The woman had made a life of feeding hungry kids—food and love.

"I'm glad she's coming back," she said. "CJ has been asking about her. He wants his grampa to meet his gramma. I think he thinks they should be married like other kids' grandparents are."

A millionaire and a mobster's widow? Brendan chuckled.

"I'm really glad that you're still here," she said.

His heart warmed, filling with hope. Did she have the same feelings he had?

"I owe you an apology," Josie said. "It was all my fault—all of it. And my mistakes cost you three years with your son." Her voice cracked. "And I am so sorry...."

He closed his arms around her and pulled her against his chest—against his heart. She trembled, probably with exhaustion and shock. She had been through so much. She clutched at his back and laid her head on his shoulder.

"My father knew who you were," she remarked. "What you were. From his sources within the FBI, he knew you were an agent. If I'd told him what story I was working on when the attempts started on my life, he would have told me to drop it—that there was no way you could be responsible. I should have known...."

"He knew?" Brendan had really underestimated the media mogul in resources and respect. He could be trusted with the truth, so Brendan should have trusted his daughter, too.

"He's a powerful man with a lot of connections," she said, "but still he didn't know that I wasn't dead. I hate that I did that to him. I hate what I did to you. I understand why you can't trust me."

"Josie..."

She leaned back and pressed her fingers over his lips. "It's okay," she said. "I understand now that sometimes it's better to leave secrets secret. There will be no stories about you or your mother in any Jessup publications or broadcasts. And there will never be another story by me."

"Never?"

Tears glistened in her smoky-green eyes, and she shook her head. "I should have never…"

"Revealed the truth?" he asked.

"Look what the consequences were," she reminded him with a shudder.

"Yes," he agreed, and finally he looked at the full picture, at what she'd really done. "You got justice for your friend—the girl that kid assaulted. If you hadn't written that article, it never would have happened. And I know from experience that it's damn hard to move on if you never get justice."

"That's why you went after all those crime organizations," she said, "to get justice for what your dad did to your mom."

"She gave up her justice for me," he said.

"So you got it for her and for so many others."

He shook his head. "No, Margaret got it for her. Go figure. But *you* helped your friend when no one else would. You can't blame yourself for what the boy did. And neither should his father."

"He needs someone to blame," she said.

Just as the people in her new town had blamed her for her student's death. Someone always needed someone else to blame.

"And so did I," she added. "I shouldn't have blamed you."

"You shouldn't have," he agreed. "Because I would have never hurt you, then or now." He dragged in a deep breath to say what he'd waited around to tell her, what he'd waited four years to tell her. "Because I love you, Josie."

"You love me?" She asked the question as if it had never occurred to her, as if she had never dared to hope. Until now. Her eyes widened with hope and revealed her own feelings.

"Yes," he said, "I love your passion and your intelligence and—"

She stretched up his body and pressed a kiss to his lips. "I didn't think you'd ever be able to trust me, much less love me."

"I don't just love you," he said. "I want to spend my life with you and CJ. No more undercover. I'll find a safer way to get justice for others, like maybe helping you with stories."

She smiled. "That might be more dangerous than your old job."

"We'll keep each other safe," he promised. "Will you become my wife?"

"It will thrill CJ if his parents are together, if every day is like that day at my house," she said.

That had been such a good day—a day Brendan had never wanted to end. His heart beat fast with hope. She was going to say yes....

"But as much as I love our son, I won't marry you for his sake," she said. "And you wouldn't want me to."

He wasn't so sure about that. But before he could argue with her, she was speaking again.

"I will marry you," she assured him, "because I love you with all my heart. Because even when I was stupid enough to think you were a bad man, I couldn't stop loving you. And I never will."

"Never," he agreed. And he covered her mouth with his, sealing their engagement with a kiss since he had yet to buy a ring. But it was no simple kiss. With them, it never was. Passion ignited and the kiss deepened.

If not for the dinging of the elevator, they might have forgotten where they were. His mother stepped through the open doors, her eyes glinting with amusement as if she'd caught him making out on the porch swing.

"We're getting married, Mom," he said.

"Of course," she said, as if there had never been any question in her mind. "Now, open the door for me." She juggled a tray of plates and coffee cups and a sippy cup.

He opened the door to his son, who threw his arms around Brendan's legs. "Daddy! Daddy, you're still here."

"I'm never leaving," he promised his son.

"Gramma!" the little boy exclaimed, and he pulled away from Brendan to follow her to his grandfather's bedside.

With a happy sigh, Josie warned him, "We're never going to have a moment alone."

"Our honeymoon," he said. "We'll spend our honeymoon alone."

Epilogue

"We're alone," Brendan said as he carried Josie over the threshold of their private suite.

Since his arms were full with her and her overflowing gown, she swung the door closed behind them. It shut with a click, locking them in together. "Yes, we're finally alone...."

And she didn't want to waste a minute of their wedding night, so she wriggled in his arms, the way their independent son did because he thought himself too big to be carried. As she slid down Brendan's body, he groaned as if in pain.

"Was I too heavy?" she asked.

He shook his head. "No, you're perfect—absolutely perfect." He lifted his fingers to her hair, which was piled in red ringlets atop her head. "You looked like a princess coming down the aisle of the ballroom."

"Well, technically..." She was. It had made her an anomaly growing up, so she'd often downplayed her mother's royal heritage. When she'd married Stanley Jessup, her mother had given up her title anyway. But here it was no big deal. Josie was only one of three princesses in the palace on St. Pierre Island. Four, actually, counting Charlotte Green-Timmer's new daughter.

Charlotte and Aaron had married shortly before their daughter's premature birth.

There was a prince, too—Gabriella and Whit Howell's baby boy. The princess had fallen in love with and married her father's other royal bodyguard. There were so many babies…

So much love. But she'd felt the most coming from her husband as he'd waited for her father to lead her down the aisle to him. In his tuxedo, the same midnight-black as his hair, he looked every bit the prince. Or a king.

And standing at his side, in a miniature replica of his father's tuxedo, had stood their son—both ring bearer, with the satin pillow in his hand, and best little man.

"It was the most perfect day," she said. A day she had thought would never come—not four years ago when she'd had to die, all those times she nearly had died, and during the three months it had taken to plan the wedding.

"As hard as you and my mom worked on it," he said, "it was guaranteed to be perfect."

She blinked back tears at the fun she'd had planning the wedding with Roma. "Your mother is amazing."

"She's your mother, too, now," he reminded her.

And the tears trickled out. "I feel that way." That she truly had a mother now. "And my dad loves you like a son." He couldn't have been prouder than to have his daughter marry a hero like FBI Agent Brendan O'Hannigan.

"I'm glad," Brendan said. "But right now I don't want to talk about your dad or my mom." He stepped closer to her, as if closing in on a suspect. "I don't want to talk at all."

Her tears quickly dried as she smiled in anticipation. "Oh, what would you rather do?"

"Get you the hell out of this dress," he said as he stared down at the yards of white lace and satin.

With its sweetheart neckline, long sleeves and flowing train, it was a gown fit for a princess—or so his mother had convinced her. Josie was glad, though, because she had wanted something special for this special day. A gown that she could one day pass down to a daughter.

"Your mom told the seamstress to put in a zipper," she told him. "She said her son was too impatient for buttons."

He grinned and reached for the tab. The zipper gave a metallic sigh as he released it, and the weight of the fabric pulled down the gown. She stood before her husband in nothing but a white lace bra and panties.

"You're the one wearing too many clothes now," she complained and reached for his bow tie.

He shrugged off his jacket, and for once he wore no holsters beneath it. He carried no guns. When their honeymoon was over, he would, but as a supervising agent, he wouldn't often have occasion to use them. He wasn't going undercover anymore—except with her.

She pulled back the blankets on the bed as he quickly discarded the rest of his clothes. "In a hurry?" she teased.

"I don't know how much time we'll have before CJ shows up," he admitted.

"His grandparents promised to keep him busy for the next couple of days," she reminded him. "And he's more fascinated with the royal babies right now than he is with us."

Brendan grinned and reached for her.

"He wants one, you know," Josie warned.

Brendan kissed her softly, tenderly, and admitted in a whisper, "So do I."

She regretted all that her unfounded suspicions had cost him—seeing her pregnant, feeling their son kick, seeing him born, holding him as a sweet-smelling infant...

But she would make it up to him with more babies—and with all her love. She tugged her naked husband down onto the bed with her. "Then we better get busy..."

Building their family and their lives together.

* * * * *

COMING NEXT MONTH from Harlequin® Intrigue®

AVAILABLE APRIL 23, 2013

#1419 THE MARSHAL'S HOSTAGE

The Marshals of Maverick County

Delores Fossen

Marshal Dallas Walker is none too happy to learn his old flame, Joelle Tate, is reopening a cold case where he is one of her prime suspects.

#1420 SPECIAL FORCES FATHER

The Delancey Dynasty

Mallory Kane

A Special Forces operative and a gutsy psychiatrist must grapple with a ruthless kidnapper—and their unflagging mutual attraction—to save the child she never wanted him to know about.

#1421 THE PERFECT BRIDE

Sutton Hall Weddings

Kerry Connor

To uncover the truth about her friend's death, Jillian Jones goes undercover as a bride-to-be at a mysterious mansion, soon drawing the suspicions of the manor's darkly handsome owner—and the attention of a killer....

#1422 EXPLOSIVE ATTRACTION

Lena Diaz

A serial bomber fixates on Dr. Darby Steele and only police detective Rafe Morgan can help her. Together they try to figure out how she became the obsession of a madman before she becomes the next victim.

#1423 PROTECTING THEIR CHILD

Angi Morgan

Texas Ranger Cord McCrea must escape through the west Texas mountains with his pregnant ex-wife to stay one step ahead of the deadly gunman who has targeted his entire family.

#1424 BODYGUARD LOCKDOWN

Donna Young

Booker McKnight has sworn revenge on the man who killed fifty men—Booker's men. His bait? The only woman he's ever loved. The problem? She doesn't know.

You can find more information on upcoming Harlequin® titles, free excerpts and more at www.Harlequin.com.

REQUEST YOUR FREE BOOKS!
2 FREE NOVELS PLUS 2 FREE GIFTS!

◆HARLEQUIN®

INTRIGUE®

BREATHTAKING ROMANTIC SUSPENSE

YES! Please send me 2 FREE Harlequin Intrigue® novels and my 2 FREE gifts (gifts are worth about $10). After receiving them, if I don't wish to receive any more books, I can return the shipping statement marked "cancel." If I don't cancel, I will receive 6 brand-new novels every month and be billed just $4.49 per book in the U.S. or $5.24 per book in Canada. That's a savings of at least 14% off the cover price! It's quite a bargain! Shipping and handling is just 50¢ per book in the U.S. and 75¢ per book in Canada.* I understand that accepting the 2 free books and gifts places me under no obligation to buy anything. I can always return a shipment and cancel at any time. Even if I never buy another book, the two free books and gifts are mine to keep forever.

182/382 HDN FVQV

Name	(PLEASE PRINT)
Address	Apt. #
City	State/Prov. Zip/Postal Code

Signature (if under 18, a parent or guardian must sign)

Mail to the **Harlequin® Reader Service:**
IN U.S.A.: P.O. Box 1867, Buffalo, NY 14240-1867
IN CANADA: P.O. Box 609, Fort Erie, Ontario L2A 5X3
**Are you a subscriber to Harlequin Intrigue books
and want to receive the larger-print edition?
Call 1-800-873-8635 or visit www.ReaderService.com.**

* Terms and prices subject to change without notice. Prices do not include applicable taxes. Sales tax applicable in N.Y. Canadian residents will be charged applicable taxes. Offer not valid in Quebec. This offer is limited to one order per household. Not valid for current subscribers to Harlequin Intrigue books. All orders subject to credit approval. Credit or debit balances in a customer's account(s) may be offset by any other outstanding balance owed by or to the customer. Please allow 4 to 6 weeks for delivery. Offer available while quantities last.

Your Privacy—The Harlequin® Reader Service is committed to protecting your privacy. Our Privacy Policy is available online at www.ReaderService.com or upon request from the Harlequin Reader Service.

We make a portion of our mailing list available to reputable third parties that offer products we believe may interest you. If you prefer that we not exchange your name with third parties, or if you wish to clarify or modify your communication preferences, please visit us at www.ReaderService.com/consumerschoice or write to us at Harlequin Reader Service Preference Service, P.O. Box 9062, Buffalo, NY 14269. Include your complete name and address.

HI13

SPECIAL EXCERPT FROM

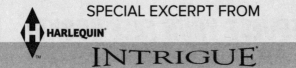

HARLEQUIN

INTRIGUE

THE MARSHAL'S HOSTAGE
by USA TODAY *bestselling author*

Delores Fossen

A sexy U.S. marshal and a feisty bride-to-be must go on
the run when danger from their past resurfaces....

"Where the hell do you think you're going?" Dallas demanded.

But he didn't wait for an answer. He hurried to her, hauled her onto his shoulder caveman-style and carried her back into the dressing room.

That's when she saw the dark green Range Rover squeal to a stop in front of the church.

Owen.

Joelle struggled to get out of Dallas's grip, but he held on and turned to see what had captured her attention. Owen, dressed in a tux, stepped from the vehicle and walked toward his men. She had only seconds now to defuse this mess.

"I have to talk to him," she insisted.

"No. You don't," Dallas disagreed.

Joelle groaned because that was the pigheaded tone she'd encountered too many times to count.

"I'll be the one to talk to Owen," Dallas informed her. "I want to find out what's going on."

Joelle managed to slide out of his grip and put her feet on the floor. She latched on to his arm to stop him from going to the door. "You can't. You have no idea how bad things can get if you do that."

He stopped, stared at her. "Does all of this have something to do with your report to the governor?"

She blinked, but Joelle tried to let that be her only reaction. "No."

"Are you going to tell me what this is all about?" Dallas demanded.

"I can't. It's too dangerous." Joelle was ready to start begging him to leave. But she didn't have time to speak.

Dallas hooked his arm around her, lifted her and tossed her back over his shoulder.

"What are you doing?" Joelle tried to get away, tried to get back on her feet, but he held on tight.

Dallas threw open the dressing room door and started down the hall with her. "I'm kidnapping you."

Be sure to pick up
THE MARSHAL'S HOSTAGE
by USA TODAY *bestselling author Delores Fossen,*
on sale April 23 wherever
Harlequin Intrigue books are sold!